MY
WICKED
HEART

USA TODAY BESTSELLING AUTHOR
T.L. SMITH

CHAPTER
1

Rylee

Rhianna's soft hands wipe at my face. She's worried. She wants my tears to stop. But how do you make your heart stop bleeding?

I haven't figured that out yet.

It's been five days since I last saw him.

Heard from him.

Touched him.

He was at the police station.

They cleared him.

He left.

He. Just. Left.

Noah won't tell me where he is. Rhianna has even tried to get the location from him.

Noah knows, and he's keeping it a secret, or he doesn't—I can't be sure which one.

Either way, I'm mad. So damn mad.

Rhianna stays next to me. She has been by my side for the last five days. I should feel sorry for Noah that I am hogging her time. But I need her. I really need her right now.

The door to the room flies open, and Beckham stands in front of us, his eyes red and his face stone cold. Without thinking, I reach for him, but he steps back, shaking his head. Beckham never steps back from me, maybe from Rhianna but never from me.

"Beckham."

His head lifts and his eyes fall on me, then they turn into angry slits.

"Beckham." Rhianna rises from the bed and steps over to me. We both stand in front of him. "What happened?" she asks.

We hear the door to the apartment open. Noah comes straight to where we are in my doorway. His eyes fall to Beckham before they shift to Rhianna and me.

"What's going on?" Rhianna asks.

"She's dead," Beckham says. I've never heard him so angry before. So ... volatile.

"Who?" I ask as Rhianna sucks in a breath next to me.

Noah walks in, pushing past Beckham while I stare at him.

"Beckham, I..." I have no words. The tears that leave my eyes now are not for August but for the young boy standing in front of me. "Beckham," I say again, reaching for him. He shakes his head and steps back once more, so I can't touch him.

"They couldn't save her. After five days, they couldn't save her," he screams. "She slipped away with her fragile hand stuck in mine." He says the last part in a whisper.

Since that day, Paige had been in the hospital, and she lost so much blood they had to give her more. Which caused an infection.

I had hopes she would be fine—she was young and healthy.

I guessed wrong.

So wrong.

"Beckham," I repeat his name and reach for him. Not letting him get away from me this time, I throw my arms around his neck and hug him tight. He loved her. He and Paige had something beautiful. Being friends first, their love turned into something special. Even my mother liked Paige, knowing who she was and where she came from.

She was good for Beckham.

"Rylee, let me go," Beckham says. I drop my arms from around his neck, and he takes a step back. "August was there as well," he says, and his words are like a punch in the gut. "He may have been cleared, but I'm pretty sure he's going to find Josh and pull him from the grave simply to beat his ass." Beckham smirks.

I'm not sure if he's being truthful or exaggerating. I haven't seen August to know. He refuses to see me, even when they held him at the station while they investigated. Thankfully, Glenn got there early enough to see most of it, and it was an open and shut case. They were thankful to have Josh off the streets, but also, August was there, and he shouldn't have been.

I turn to see Rhianna's head on Noah's chest as he strokes her hair to calm her down.

"Where is he?" I ask. Noah's hand pauses for a second, it's so quick I almost miss it, and then he shakes his head. "Just tell me where he is. His sister died," I yell at him.

"Last I heard he was heading to Josh's house." I look back at Beckham and see him watching Noah with sad eyes. Noah shakes his head at

Beckham but doesn't say anything.

"Do you want to come?" I ask Beckham.

Beckham's hands slide into his pockets, and he nods his head once.

"No, Rylee. Stay here." Rhianna pulls herself from Noah's arms and reaches for me. I don't let her.

"I have to go," I reply.

"No, you do not," she says, her voice higher than usual. "You don't know what you're about to walk in on. Stop and think."

"No. I've stopped and thought. I need to go." I walk out of my room and snatch my keys from the kitchen counter. Beckham is right behind me as I keep walking until we reach the car.

"Rylee." We both turn to see Glenn, Paige's father, standing there. Glenn has sunglasses covering his eyes, so I can't see the pain that I know will be radiating off of him, but I can feel it. "Beckham, where are you going?"

I turn to look at Beckham. His jaw is stiff as he grinds his teeth.

"It wasn't his fault. You know this," Glenn says.

I look between the two and grimace at the uncertain tone.

"Beckham," I say his name, but he doesn't look at me.

He keeps his focus on Glenn. "It is his fault. It's *all* his fault," Beckham says through clenched teeth.

Glenn shakes his head then steps closer to Beckham. "No, it's not. It's not his fault at all." Glenn's hand touches Beckham's shoulder, and I am afraid I'm missing the point here.

"Glenn?" I ask, stepping around the car.

"You should go, Rylee. Beckham won't be going with you." I look at Beckham. Confusion is written all over my face, so much so I am sure my eyebrows are touching.

"Beckham," I say, and he scrunches up his nose.

"It's his fault, Rylee," he repeats.

"Whose?" I ask, still not understanding.

Glenn goes to speak, but Beckham cuts him off before he can. "It's all August's fault. All. Of. It."

Oh. Oh ... shit.

"I..." What do I even say? "It's Josh's fault, not August's, Beckham," I manage to reply.

"You can't see it because you are blinded in your relationship." Beckham leans in, and his voice high when he screams, "You can't see it."

I take a step back.

That hurt, a lot.

My baby brother is so angry. His pain and hurt radiate from him with such force, I'm afraid he's going to loathe me for loving August.

I can't lose Beckham.

"She's right. It's not his fault, Beckham. Come with me. Come on." Glenn turns Beckham, and they start walking away to his car. I watch as Beckham leaves, not looking my way at all. Glenn only gives me a curt nod as they drive off, and I am left standing next to my car, wondering what I should do.

A part of me is screaming to get in the car and go.

To see what he's doing.

See how he's doing.

The other is telling me to turn around, walk back inside, curl myself in bed, and not move.

I shake my head. No, I've done that. Now I have to get in and see him because, clearly, he won't come find me.

Somehow, I manage to start the car. With steady hands, I drive to where I believe August is located. When I come to a stop out the front, the door is open. Stepping out of the car, no sounds are coming from inside. I close the car door, hugging my arms around my body for comfort as I stand at the entrance.

It's cold.

Why is it so cold?

"August," I yell for him in hope he's here and I don't have to step inside. But when no one answers, I walk through the doorway and instantly have to cover my nose.

Oh, holy hell, what is that stink?

It smells bad.

"August," I say again, walking farther in. I hear a muffled noise and step over many bottles strewn over the floor as I make my way to what I am guessing is the living room.

"Leave," a voice booms.

I search for the source but cannot find it. I know it's August, though. I'd know that voice anywhere just like the back of my hand.

It whispers to me in my dreams.

I love that voice.

Muffled sounds are heard again, and I step over more shit on the floor until I come face-to-face with August. His hair is a mess. His face is stricken with anger, and his hands are bunched to his sides, one of them gripping a knife. When I listen, muffled noises are heard again, so I glance past August to the two men who are lying on the floor, both of them gagged and tied. Blood is seeping from multiple wounds, and it's pooling on the carpet beneath them.

"August," I say again and step closer.

"I said *fucking leave,* Rylee. What part of that don't you understand?" he screams.

"Beckham blames you," I blurt out. I don't know why I said it, but for some reason, it's the only thing that leaves my mouth.

"Good," he says, his hand clenching the knife so hard he is white-knuckling it.

"What do you plan to do with that?" I ask, my eyes flicking to the blade glinting in the dim light.

He smirks, and it's not your average smirk. It's more sinister. Actually, it's more like a sneer.

"You should leave before you find out," August says, not taking his forest green eyes off me.

"Your sister," I say solemnly.

"Is dead ... I know." He says it with calm certainty, and I wonder who this person is standing in front of me. He seems to be void of all emotion. I haven't seen this side of him before, and I'm not sure what's caused him to be this way.

"You should come back with me," I say.

"Not gonna happen, rich girl. You and me, we were a fantasy that has now burst. So, leave before you get in trouble."

One of the guys on the floor starts to move, and my eyes fall to him. He looks familiar.

"Who is that?"

"Just an ant that needs to be exterminated."

My head shakes automatically at his words. "He was one of the guys in your house," I declare, realization hitting me. "August, what are you doing?"

"Rich girl ... *fucking leave*." He turns away from me and goes to the man who's looking my way. He grabs him by the hair and pulls him up on his knees and brings the knife to his neck. August looks back at me and smiles. "Last chance, rich girl. You should leave before your soul is tainted forever."

"My soul isn't perfect," I profess, watching the knife cut into the man's skin, his blood now pooling around the blade.

"No, I guess I tainted it, didn't I," he says, smiling, showing his teeth. Then, in one swift movement, he cuts the guy's neck and lets him drop to the floor with a thud.

What the actual fuck?

CHAPTER 2

Rylee

I should be screaming, yelling, crying. But I've done enough of that over the last few days. Seeing August standing there, the knife still in hand, I can't seem to walk away.

Am I a sucker for the wrong man?

Anderson was a prime example of my poor decision making.

But August, well, he's different.

Not once have I thought he would touch me in ways that could hurt me. I feel safe with him. I know what the devil looks like, and he is not him.

Even if what I'm witnessing says otherwise.

Maybe I'm brainwashed—fucked in the head.

But something in me is telling me he's a good man.

"Rich girl, *leave,*" he says again, this time on a growl.

"Do you want to go back to prison?" I ask.

August pauses while looking down at the guy on the floor.

"Don't, August. Please, think about what you're doing. Is it worth it?"

"They won't know it was me. How do you think Josh got away free for so long? I have all his connections now, and all of them..." he pauses, looks back over his shoulder at me, "... are scared of me. I warned him I would come for him, and he didn't listen. The reason he sent me to jail and didn't kill me was so he could prove he had power over me."

He takes a beat before continuing, "He didn't. And I've proven that now." His foot lifts, and he rams it down on the guy at his feet.

"August." I say his name in the hopes he will turn around and walk away.

"This is one of the guys who took her ... who gave her to him," he says, pressing more weight on him with his foot. "Go *now,* Rylee. You need to leave."

"You've said that before."

August removes his foot from the guy and walks over to me. The hand that held the knife rises, and he touches my face with it, stroking gently, then takes a deep breath. "You are the most beautiful thing I have ever seen," he whispers, leaning down to kiss me, and I allow it because I am defenseless and vulnerable to his touch.

Every. Single. Time.

His lips push against mine with enough pressure. It's all I can feel. August moves close, so close that no air can come between us.

He takes, and I let him.

I don't need to breathe when he's so willing to give me his breath.

When he pulls back and I open my eyes, he's watching me.

"Now *fucking leave* and never come back. If you try to find me, rich girl, your brother will come, and I *will* have to defend myself. Do you want to lose your brother as well?"

August's words hit me hard.

So hard I take a step back. He nods once in acknowledgment, turning and walking to the guy on the floor.

"It was fun while it lasted, rich girl," he says without so much as a final glance at me.

It takes me a moment to compose myself, and when I do, I turn and walk out of the door and out of that house. When I reach my car, my hands are shaking violently. My reflection shines back at me from the car window. There's smudged blood over my face. I wipe it off and shake my head.

Getting in the car, I call my brother, but he doesn't pick up.

So I call Rhianna. She picks up immediately.

"Where is Beckham?" I ask.

"Still with Glenn, I'm pretty sure."

"Okay, thanks."

"Ry, he blames August. You should stay away from August, okay? At least until Beckham has time to heal ... time to think about things. I'm afraid of what might happen."

She isn't wrong. Beckham is almost an adult. He's in his last year of high school, and after that, well, I don't even know what's going to happen.

He made plans with Paige, and now...

Well, fuck.

After spinning my wheels, I drive off again trying to compose myself. Once I have everything under control and my mind on a better track, I stop at the local ice cream parlor, where I know August's friend, Sully, works. Before I get out of the car, I check my face in the mirror and then head inside. I spot him right away.

"Rylee," he says, raising an eyebrow. I guess he's shocked to see me.

Luckily he's not serving a customer, so I march straight to the counter. Sully nods and steps out, so I follow him to the back of the shop, then wait for him to stop before I speak, "Can we talk?"

"What's going on?" he asks.

I look around to make sure no one is about before I open my mouth.

"It's clear. It's just me today."

"I need you to go to August. He's..."

"Fallen off the deep end?" he finishes.

I nod. "Yes, very much so."

"August's always been a man with no fear. He did most things with a vengeance, but after he got out of jail, he changed and became calmer," he states.

"He is anything but calm now."

"I don't think there's much I can do."

I groan at his words. "He's at Josh's house, with two others..." I pause. "One was still alive when I left."

"August can be good, Rylee, but he can also be incredibly bad. How do you think he has survived all that he has?"

"I can't be the one to help him. My brother..."

He flinches. "It's fine, I'll go. I just can't promise anything."

I nod. It's all I can do.

No one can promise me the stars. If I wanted them, I know I would need to get them myself. I turn to walk out when Sully calls my name.

"If it means anything, I've never seen him with anyone the way he was with you."

It's like a punch to my already bruised gut.

"Thank you," I say, holding back my tears, I continue to walk out.

I've cried enough to last me a lifetime. I don't want to cry anymore.

When I get back to my apartment, my mother is there, her hands on her hips as she looks around.

"Where is Rhi..."

"Where have you been?" Her hands don't drop as she stares at me.

"What's it matter?" I bite back.

Mom nods to my room, and I take a step in that direction. Opening the door quietly, I find Beckham asleep on my bed.

"I gave him something to sleep. He needs the rest." His face looks so angry, even when he sleeps.

I turn as my mother pulls out a chair at the table.

"Sit, we need to talk." I do as she says, as if on autopilot. Her hands come to rest on the table after she sits, then she leans in slightly to look me over.

"Mother."

"You haven't been eating. You've lost weight," she says.

Appearances are all she cares about, so I keep my lips sealed, not wanting to argue.

"Aside from Paige, Beckham was closest to you, so I thought it was best I bring him here." I look away from her again to my brother, who's asleep on my bed. "He's hurting. Paige was a good girl, and I'm afraid of how this may change him," Mom says, biting her lip when I look back at her.

"Why do you care?" I ask with venom in my tone. I'm not sure why it left my mouth in that manner, and my mother is as surprised as I am by my outburst.

"He's my baby. Will always be my baby." She goes quiet. "As you will always be my girl."

The door opens, and my sister and Noah walk in.

"Umm, hello, what's going on?" Rhianna walks over to me, places a hand on my shoulder, and then looks down at our mother.

"No need to come to the defense of your sister, Rhianna. I am her mother." Our mother's glaring eyes fall to Rhianna.

"If you say so," Rhianna replies, not removing her hand from me in some sort of comfort move as she eyes our mother.

My mom stands, walks over and looks into my room, then back to me. "Call me if Beckham needs me. Hopefully, he gets some sleep while I plan the funeral. I told Glenn not to worry, that I'm going to take care of it all."

"That's awfully nice of you, Poppy," Noah says.

Rhianna coughs and gives him a solid glare. Noah doesn't shy away from her, just offers her a small twitch of his lips before Poppy walks out the door leaving us be.

When the door clicks shut, Rhianna turns to Noah with her hands on her hips, and the look on her face is priceless.

"What?" he asks, now in a full smile.

"Gosh, I'm gonna have to put something in your coffee for sure now," she says seriously, and Noah laughs.

We hear a groan, and we all turn to Beckham who's sitting up on the bed. He's rubbing his head as we walk into my room.

"Mom?" Beckham asks, looking past us.

"She left," Rhianna tells him.

"She gave me something." He looks up. "It's not a dream?" he asks, then lays back down, closing his eyes.

Rhianna's eyes are squinted in concern. This is the type of heartbreak we wouldn't wish on anyone.

"Leave him be. Time is the only thing that heals."

We turn to Noah who's looking down at the floor. Rhianna reaches for him and places her hand in his.

"It's his first love. It will take time to get over losing her the way he did."

I nod, knowing Noah would know precisely how Beckham feels. He lost his wife, and he was lucky enough to find love again with my sister.

We step out of the room and shut the door this time, giving Beckham privacy and time to grieve.

Rhianna stays next to Noah, who looks down at me sympathetically.

"How is August?"

I look away. It's all I can do. I have no words to adequately describe my feelings regarding him.

It hurts too much.

And there is enough hurt happening in this apartment right now.

CHAPTER
3

August

They say when your happiest moment happens, if you're lucky, it can last hours, days even. Mine was simply a moment. My life is nothing but made up of moments.

When I was ten, I had to dig through the trash bin to find myself something to eat. When I was eleven, I had to steal for the first time, as my shoes no longer fitted me. Then when I was seventeen, I realized my strength.

But my most significant moment, the one I know I will always cherish?

It was her.

Will always be her.

Her dark, soulless eyes and those pink, plush lips pull me in.

Even now, as I stand over the last man who had a hand in giving my sister to Josh, I wonder if this is another moment.

But it's not.

This was inevitable.

He was bound to die, and by my hands at that.

"August."

I don't turn.

I know who it is straight away.

And I've run out of fucks to give.

"Rylee is concerned," he says.

I glance down at the guy below me. I don't even know his name.

Do I care?

No.

I fucking do not.

His face is a bloody mess, his eyes are swollen shut from all the hits he's taken. Sully doesn't even seem to care that a man is lying dead at his feet and another is almost there.

"Rylee will always be concerned," I tell him.

"It's just who she is."

"You love her."

"What is love? Because we've never been shown it to know it. So, what is it?" I turn away from the guy at my feet and look Sully dead in the eyes. He flinches and averts his eyes almost immediately.

"You'll discover that it takes time. It took time with me, but I got there."

"You're lying. You still think you're unlovable and wondering when he will realize it as well."

Sully's eyes go wide at my words. Concern flashes in them before he shakes it away. "I know what you're doing, August. You're hurt, so now you're lashing out. Don't fuck it up so you never get a chance again. I'm not sure Noah can save you from this."

"I don't need saving, Sully. I fucking don't." I turn, reaching for the gun I know Josh keeps hidden in the recliner and smile as my hand glides over the cool metal. I pull it out and squat down so I can pick up the dude's head.

"You fucked with the wrong person, and now you *will* pay the price," I seethe then put the gun to his skull before I pull the trigger. He's dead instantly, his head falling like a bag of shit, brain matter and blood going everywhere. I reach out and wipe my hands on his shirt before standing.

"August." Sully shakes his head, his eyes wide

with horror. He's seen death before, but he thought I would stop. He was dead wrong.

"No need to worry, Sully. I was never here." I smile and light a cigarette. "You better leave before it all blows up in your face."

Sully's eyes dart around the room, and it's then he sees the fuel before his gaze lands back on me. "They will know it's you."

"They'll have trouble figuring that out considering all the evidence points to Josh."

"You—"

"*Go,* Sully. This house will light up the sky in five minutes." I smile, pulling the cigarette from my lips. "Sully, *go.* Now!"

He nods reluctantly, and I watch as he leaves. Then I sit in the recliner and look around at this shithole I once called home. Now I see it for what it truly is, a prison which I am now free from. I'm not sure which one I'm more relieved to be free of, this one or the penitentiary.

Standing, I start splashing the fuel everywhere and wiping anywhere I touched just to be safe. I leave the plastic covering my shoes on before I tear off my shirt and throw on a clean one as I walk to the back door.

The house's back leads into the woods, and I don't plan to go around the front where other people can see me.

My phone rings in my pocket, and I have to close my eyes to the sound of it.

It's the ringtone Paige set for Rylee.

Some shit about love.

I tried to be a better man.

I really did. For them. For her.

But I think once you know who you really are, there is no escaping it. I am not a good man. I am anything but. I am my mother's son, and these hands have seen death and taken life multiple times. I doubt this will be the last.

I light a match and throw it, stepping out of the house I once called home. A place that fed me, gave me money, and helped me survive. But also, one that trapped me in its clutches.

Burn, you fucking whore. Burn.

CHAPTER
4

Rylee

"You've heard the news?" Rhianna asks while sitting next to me. Today is Paige's funeral and marks three days since I last saw August.

"The house?" I ask.

She simply nods in answer.

Two days ago, that was all I heard about. How two bodies were discovered—one of them I watched die—and the house ablaze.

"I figured you would know about that. Know that he may be coming. Are you okay with that?"

"It was his sister, Rhi. Would you be okay if I didn't come to your funeral?" I bite back at her.

"No, but you know that's not what I meant. I meant will *you* be okay."

I shrug, standing in my black heels and a black dress. It's tight-fitting, but it's the only thing I could find in my closet that was remotely appropriate.

"Has Noah spoken to him?" I ask.

"Yes. August was questioned about the house, but he had an alibi. Two, actually." My head whips around to her. "Sully and another man. I think he's the security somewhere."

Wow, okay. I guess I should have expected that.

"Anyway, he's fine. Noah said he's laying low."

I doubt that, but I hope so.

A knock comes on the door, and we both turn to Noah standing there.

"It's time to go, ladies." We nod and follow him out. Beckham is meeting us there, as he is going with Mom and Dad. He's been distant from me lately, and I hate that fact. I hate that he doesn't think he can come and talk to me.

The drive isn't long, and when we arrive, most everyone is here. I look for August as if just the sight of him may ease my discomfort.

I'm afraid it won't, but what if it does?

I shake my head and get out of the car. My parents and Beckham are standing a little way from the car, so I head straight over and place my hands on Beckham's shoulders, pulling him in for a hug. He doesn't cuddle me back, but he does let me hold him. "I love you," I whisper before I pull away.

Rhianna slides her hand in mine as Beckham stands there dressed in his suit, his head down. He takes a deep breath, then walks to where we will be sitting, the rest of us following. We sit at the front next to Glenn. There is a seat saved next to Glenn, so I can only guess it's for August.

A woman steps over and looks at Glenn, who is too lost in his own personal pain to even notice her before she goes to sit at the back. I recognize her, though she looks a little different. It's August's mother, and who I'm guessing is Paige's as well.

"Rylee." When she says my name, I glance up. Her eyes are focused past the graves where a man is walking toward us, dressed in a black suit and dark glasses covering his eyes.

He is devastatingly beautiful.

Glenn stands and pulls him in for a brief one-arm hug, offering him the seat next to him. I hear a few people whispering, and I watch, hoping he will look my way, but he never does.

The service is beautiful. My mother did a great job. I lean my head on Beckham's shoulder as I listen to him softly cry. Though he tenses a bit, he doesn't push me off. When people start to stand, we stay seated. When others move away, we stay where we are.

"The pain," he says, and I turn to him to see him gripping his chest.

I don't know how to fix it because it's not something anyone can fix.

So instead, I wrap my arms around him, and we stay that way until we're the last people here and raindrops start falling on us, but we still don't move.

We sit.

Because that's what he needs.

And what Beckham needs, I am willing to give him.

I don't know how long we wait, how long we sit in the rain, but the sky isn't bright anymore, and the clouds hover, dripping sweet rain all over us.

"Beckham." Our father looks at both of us and nods to his son. "It's time to go now, son." Beckham looks to me.

"I have my car." I smile, but it's forced and he knows it but doesn't question me even though I am lying. Beckham's eyes are red, and his face is flushed. He needs rest and to get away from here, but I wasn't going to be the one to tell him we needed to leave. He needs to come to that realization on his own.

"You right to get home, Rylee?" our father asks, just to make sure. I nod, and he grips his hands around Beckham, and Beckham falls into him as they make their way to the car.

Our two chairs are the only ones left.

Everything else has been packed up.

The seat next to me squeaks, and I turn to see August. I look past him to make sure my brother is gone before I give him my full attention.

I can't help myself.

I can't stop myself.

My hands reach for his face, my body leans in, and my lips make a connection with his. I kiss him with everything I have left under the night's sky.

He doesn't kiss me back at first, just lets me kiss him until his hands find my face and he grips it hard. His fingers dig into the side of my cheeks, bruising as he does, while his lips punish me.

For what, I'm not aware.

But I'm helpless to stop him.

August's tongue slides against mine, and it's

like a bonfire of feelings ignite.

Pain.

Hurt.

Love.

Lust.

Need.

Want.

One of them stands out more than the others, but I know all of these feelings are valid.

I pull back first, breaking his lips from mine but keeping close. His hands stay on my face as his forest green eyes find mine.

"Rich girl," he says with a sad smile.

"August," I say back in barely a whisper.

The rain continues to fall around us, but neither of us seems to care.

"Where have you been?" I ask. He drops his hands and turns to look at the grave.

"Tidying up business," he says. "I'm leaving in a month, once all this is done and dusted."

My heart rate picks up at his words.

Leaving. Me.

Holy shit.

No.

No.

My hands start feeling hot, and I place them in my lap, staring at the ground.

"I'll go with you," I say in a low voice.

"No can do, rich girl. I'm a fucked-up man, and I would never take you from the people you love." He pauses. "It wouldn't be fair," he finishes.

"This isn't fair," I reply. I want him to look at me, but his gaze remains locked in front of him.

"Life isn't fair. I've known this for a long time."

"Where do you plan to go?" I ask.

"Anywhere but here. There were only ever two good things here. And one of them just left me." His eyes shift to where she's buried, and a lone tear travels down his cheek. He may think I can't see it because of the rain, but I do.

"The other isn't enough to keep you here?" I try. I would beg if I thought it would change anything.

"I would do nothing but destroy the other's life, and that is not something I would be willing to do, rich girl."

"Fuck it up. Destroy it. I don't care," I say in a loud, manic voice. He reaches for me, pulls me from the chair, and brings me to his lap.

"Tsk tsk, rich girl, you have a life … a good one. You don't need it destroyed. Think of me as a moment in time," he says, and I shake my head at his words. "You were my favorite moment in time if that's any consolation." A flash of lightning streaks across the sky.

"I don't want to be a moment, August."

He reaches up, pushes a strand of hair out of my face. "It's all we get."

I lean in and lay my head on his chest, taking him all in, as much as I can possibly take.

He's leaving me.

In a month.

"My mother is here," he says as I pull back. She's standing under a tree, getting wet but smoking a cigarette. I push off August but stay close to him as he stands. She walks over to us, putting the cigarette out as she does until she's standing in front of us. August's hands are in fists at his sides as he bites his bottom lip in anger.

"Do you want time here by yourself?" I ask.

She turns to me, squinting. "No," she declares, then looks back to August. "I came to see you. Are you okay?" she asks, and he laughs. Laughs so loud that I startle. "August." He stops when she says his name.

"You need to leave before I lay you next to

her," August spits at her.

She doesn't seem shocked by his words. At all!

"It's not my fault. I had nothing to do with it."

August screams, "You had everything to do with it. *Everything.*"

She takes a step back. "Who even are you?" she asks. Before I can even say a word, August steps in front of me, blocking her view of me.

"She is no one you need to worry about. Now, leave. Before you end up like everyone else that's associated with Josh."

"There has been chatter, August. We know what you're doing. You're tearing apart what he built."

August leans in close to her. "Destroying it, Mother. Everything he touched."

"You'll end up back there," she whispers.

"No, I won't." August reaches for my hand, slides it in his, and starts to walk off, pulling me along with him. I turn back to see her watching where our hands are joined. She has an amused smile on her face.

"August."

"Where is your car?" he asks. When I don't answer, he stops and looks around, then turns to me. "Rich girl, where is your car?"

I shrug. "Not here." His hair is now sticking to

his face, and the water runs over his lips, making me wish I were kissing them again.

"How do you intend to get home?"

"Walk," I tell him.

August shakes his head and looks back past me, to where I am guessing his mother is still standing before he looks at me again. "You can ride with me."

"You don't have a car," I tell him.

"You're right, I don't." That's when I see the motorcycle with a helmet hanging from the handlebars. He reaches for it, places it on my head, and then leans down to strap it firmly in place.

"I've never been on a bike before," I whisper somewhat in fear.

"Nothing will happen to you with me. You should know that."

I nod because I do.

I trust him even after everything I have seen.

I trust him more than any person should.

CHAPTER 5

August

Rylee's hands wrap around my waist, and she leans her body into mine. I feel her everywhere. How am I meant to leave someone I never knew I wanted?

And believe me, I want her.

But the truth of the matter is, I shouldn't.

Her hands slip under my shirt, and her cold fingers splay across my stomach. I don't push her away or even stop her from touching me.

I want her to touch me.

But I also don't.

As we pull up to her place, Noah, Beckham, and her sister are standing out the front. They all turn, and her hands fall from my skin and pull away as we stop. She hops off and drags the helmet from her head just as Beckham starts walking toward us.

"Beckham." She says his name, but it does nothing to stop him. His feet move quickly, and his hand comes even quicker. I don't move because he does deserve to get one hit in, but that will be the only one I will allow.

When his fist connects, I hear Rylee scream. He hit me good. Firm. When my head flicks back to him, I lick my lip and taste blood. He pulls back again, ready to hit me once more, but this time, I catch his fist in my hand and push him back.

"You only get one for free," I seethe. Beckham runs at me. He's fast. I guess being athletic does that for him. But I've grown up with kids like him, been picked on by kids like him. And I have dealt with worse, much worse.

I sidestep the attack, causing him to miss and stumble past me.

Noah steps in front of Beckham and places his hand on his shoulder. "That's enough, Beckham, it's not his fault."

Beckham's eyes are almost as black as his

sister's right now as he stares at me.

"It's all his fault. She didn't even know they existed before him."

"They knew," I say. Josh knew, thanks to my mother. Beckham sneers at me, and Rylee moves to stand between us.

"He's leaving. Go inside." She points, and when she does, Beckham glares at her.

"You should have stayed away from him. Now I have to see him, and it's all your fucking fault," he screams at her. Rylee flinches and steps back.

"Beckham," Rhianna chimes, stepping up to him. He ignores her and stalks past them and past me until he reaches the street. "I'll go after him."

When Rylee turns around to face me, her eyes are red, like she's holding back tears that won't fall. Noah glances between us then walks to where his girlfriend just went, leaving us standing in the street.

"Rich girl," I say in a low voice.

"It could have worked," she says, realizing what I always knew.

We were never meant to work.

Just two opposites who, though strongly attracted, can't seem to come together on the right path.

"It could have, you know. You and me, we could have worked. If only—"

"Enough," I say, a loaded exhale coating my lips.

Her eyes find the ground, and she shakes her head. I see the tears fall then, and I step up to her because, despite everything, seeing her in pain is not something I can bear.

"Think of it this way, you're free," I tell her, my hand reaching up to touch her face, pushing back a strand of hair.

Those eyes that I know will haunt me until the day I die penetrate me when she looks at me. It's like a smack to the soul I wasn't expecting but would gladly take from her.

She pinches her lip between her teeth and rolls it before she opens her mouth again. "It's never going to work," she says in a small voice.

"No," I say, dropping my hand. "It won't."

"That hurts more than you can imagine," she says, looking past me before those eyes fall back to mine. "But losing Beckham would hurt me more, of this I know."

"I know." And I do, because losing Paige, well, that has fucked me up beyond belief. And now I don't know what to do with myself. "I would never ask you to choose. Ever. I will make that choice for you." I step back and turn, reaching for the helmet, knowing if I don't leave soon, I may never leave her.

"August," she says, and when I turn back to her, she throws herself at me, her body slamming into mine as she wraps her arms around my neck, pulling me to her so our bodies are joined, and her lips slam into mine.

This isn't like our usual kisses. This one is filled with so many goodbyes that we cannot say, so many hellos that we will never get to experience. And so many I love yous that we will never have.

I hold on to her with the same force she holds on to me and kiss her back.

Love was foreign to me before she walked into my life. It still is, a little. I never really got the chance to experience it all. But I know, with her it could have been something beautiful.

She tastes like sweet tears mixed with brutal adoration.

Pulling back, she falls from my arms, separating us as her hand reaches up and touches her lips, eyelashes fanning her face as she looks at me.

"I'll miss you, August Trouble. You and your wicked heart." When she says my last name, a small smile plays on her lips before it falls away.

I turn. No more words can leave my lips as I get on my bike. I start it, sliding on my helmet as I see her brother and sister walking back toward us. I look at her one last time and imprint her in my memory.

What a beautiful memory it is, and what a wicked heart I have.

CHAPTER 6

Rylee

Watching him leave is one of the hardest things I have done. I never wanted him to go, but when my brother walks past me, still angry, I know it's the right thing to do.

His pain should come first.

Beckham lost his first love, and at his age, that's all that matters. He can't see beyond that. He doesn't know beyond her.

Rhianna places a hand on my shoulder as she walks past, giving me a squeeze before following Beckham inside. I stand there, in my wet clothes and with bruised lips. Staring in the direction August went, wondering if he will turn back.

He shouldn't, but that doesn't stop a part of me wanting him to return.

So badly.

"Rylee." I spin around to Noah standing there, still dressed in his black suit from the funeral. "I want to give you these." He passes me a set of keys. "They're to my apartment. I have a feeling you may not want to go in there right now." He nods to my apartment. "If you just need some time, take it. I won't be back until tomorrow if you want to chill by yourself. I have wine in the fridge and chocolates in the cupboard."

"Thank you."

"He lost someone dear to him. Anger takes time before grief sets in. He loves you. It's why he is taking it out on you the most. He knows you'll be there, and you can handle it. So, just give him time." I nod. "If you need anything, call me," he says, then turns and heads inside. I reach for my keys in my purse and walk over to my car, not bothering to go inside to grab anything I might need, and leave.

If you had told me a few days ago that the person who hates me the most right now would be my brother, I would have laughed at you because that would never happen. But it did.

I spent two nights at Noah's, soaking in his bath and crying myself to sleep every night. Then I went back to work.

Shandy kept my office shut and made sure no one disturbed me. I'm thankful for her looking out for me.

Every hour, I look down at my phone and wonder if he will answer if I called.

Would he?

Where is he?

I don't have the answer to these questions, and no one has spoken about August either. It's like he never existed. But he did. My body and mind know, oh boy, do they know.

The days tend to blend into each other, and I don't go home for the rest of the week until Friday rolls around, thanks to Noah giving me extra time. I found a few extra clothes of Rhianna's at Noah's and have been wearing them for the time being. But now I have to go home to get some clothes of my own. When I open the door to my apartment, I find her waiting for me at the table. Her head raises, and her dark eyes lock on me, and she offers me a smile.

"How you doing?" she asks.

"How's Beckham?" I say, ignoring her

question.

She shrugs. "As good as he can be. He went back home yesterday. Mom came and got him. But he's refusing to go to school next week." She pauses. "But, I asked how you are. So, tell me, how are you?"

"I'm fine."

"Fine is a lie. We both know that."

I ignore her and head to my room, dropping the bag of dirty clothes I have.

"Noah hasn't spoken to him if that's any consolation," Rhianna says, following me as I start to clean up my mess. My hands pause on my bedsheets as I hear her speak of him. "And Noah said August should be fine, wherever he is."

"Yep," I answer. Of that, I don't have any doubt.

"But you are clearly not." She wraps her arms around me and pulls me to her, so my back is to her front. I let her hug me and don't move. If I do, I may just cry. "I'll order us dinner," she says, giving me one last squeeze before leaving the room. I shut the door behind her and lie on my bed. Reaching for my phone, I bring up his number.

No contact.

It would be the smart thing to do, not to speak

to him. But what if he answers?

It's been a week, and I can still taste him on my lips.

Miss him between my sheets and want him by my side.

I press call and put the phone to my ear as I listen to it ring.

He answers but doesn't say hello.

August knows it's me. *Is he not saying anything because it's me?*

I hear the rev of an engine in the background and just lie there wondering what I should say.

"I missed you today," I whisper, hearing his breathing into the phone, but he doesn't respond. "And I missed you every other day before that."

The tears fall now.

Why isn't he saying anything?

Doesn't he miss me as well?

"I haven't been home all week. I finally came home today. Beckham still won't talk to me."

I hear Rhianna call my name.

"I have to go, August," I choke out, bite my lip, and shake my head. Before I can say anything else, I hang up.

"You okay?" Rhianna asks. I nod and stand

from my bed to follow her out. When I enter the kitchen, Beckham is there, his hands at his sides as he stares at me.

"Beckham," I say, taking a step closer to him. He's taller than me now. When I look at him, I don't see a boy any longer. He's almost a man. In a few months, he'll be eighteen. He and Paige were going to live together after school.

That isn't going to happen now.

"I'm so mad at you," he says, his eyes pinning me. "But I love you." A soft, sad smile plays on my lips as I walk over and wrap my arms around him. He pushes me away. When I squeeze and hold on tighter, he finally wraps his arms around me too, and we simply stand there. Holding each other. Helping each other grieve.

"Guys, I'm starting to become the jealous sister again." I chuckle as I pull away from Beckham and shake my head. She pulls out food that I didn't even know she had ordered, and we all sit with me next to Beckham. His eyes are still so red, I want to take his burden away, but I can't. It's impossible for me to do so.

"They had his funeral last week. No one went but one woman," Beckham says to me, talking about Josh. I have a feeling I know who that one woman was.

August's mother.

"Good, he's an ass," Rhianna chimes in.

"How do you know?" I ask.

"Glenn told me," he answers straight away.

"How is Glenn?"

"On leave. He hasn't left his house."

That breaks my heart.

The door opens, and Noah walks in carrying two bottles of wine that he places on the table in front of us. My sister doesn't hesitate to open one and starts pouring me a glass, then one for herself.

"Rylee." Noah hands me a set of keys.

I look at them, confused.

"For you to get your things," he says, and Beckham shakes his head and swears next to me. It's then I realize they're the keys to August's house.

August's house, which he no longer lives in.

A part of me wants to ask Noah if he knows where he is right now.

How did he sound when he spoke to him?

Is he still as dark as that day I saw him?

Or if he's back to the August I know.

There could be two sides to him, but I can handle that. I could have, I mean. Because even when he was at his darkest, he was still trying to protect me. Looking out for me.

"Burn it," Beckham says as I slide the keys from the table, away from his angry glare.

"Also, change of subject," Rhianna says. "Anderson's baby mama cornered me the other day at the shop thinking I was you." She smirks. "She wants to apologize. She feels awful about what happened."

I shake my head. I pressed charges, and now it's up to the courts to deal with.

I have a restraining order on Anderson because I don't want him anywhere near me.

"It's none of her concern."

"She thinks it is," Rhianna says, raising an eyebrow. "Anyway, told her she had the wrong sister, and she asked me to ask you if you could meet with her. I told her she was dreaming, then left." She smiles. "You do not need to involve yourself in anything that crazy family does, and now she is attached to it. We both know you are the number one hit for his mother now you pressed charges against her precious boy." She pretends to gag on the last part.

"I'm staying away from them," I tell her.

"Good, because Mom was saying the other day that Anderson's mother has been talking shit about our family. And as you can imagine, that doesn't sit well with Mother."

"Of course it doesn't," Beckham says.

"I'm sorry," I say, turning to face him. He looks at me and shrugs.

"I'm over being angry at you."

"Tell me, why do you love her more?" Rhianna says, eyeing us both. Beckham shakes his head and starts to dig into the food while she pins me with a stare.

"I love you the most," Noah chimes in to distract her.

"I know that, but you see, I like attention. And I should be her favorite at least," Rhianna says, making Noah smile at her neediness. We all know how she is, and we love her all the same for it.

"We love you just the same," I tell her.

Rhianna pokes her tongue out and crosses her arms over her chest in defiance.

Beckham nudges me with a small smile, and Rhianna pulls a face at his action.

Maybe the days will get easier.

Or maybe they won't.

CHAPTER 7

Rylee

It's been two weeks since Noah gave me those keys, and I still haven't built up the guts to go back there. It will do nothing but remind me of him.

I'm getting better, and I can't do anything to jeopardize that. As much as I've wanted to call August again, I haven't. Even if my fingers are itching to do so.

He didn't talk last time. So what would be the chances he would if I tried again?

When I get home from work, everyone is

there—Rhianna, my parents, Noah, and Beckham.

I look around, wondering why they're all here. "What's going on?" I ask as Rhianna holds out her hand to me. I look at it, confused. Then I see it, a stunning ring sits proudly on her finger. It's an oval-shaped diamond with a band of smaller diamonds surrounding it.

"Holy shit," I say, shaking my head and smiling at her.

"I guess Mom gets to plan that wedding after all," Rhianna says with a brilliant smile that will not budge. I don't blame her. She and Noah, well, they are perfect for each other.

Pulling her in for a hug, she squeezes me back.

"You do realize you buy one, you get the other for free," Beckham says to Noah, his eyes cast on the PlayStation.

Rhianna laughs because she knows it's true, and Noah just smiles.

"Your funeral," Beckham mutters before going back to his game.

"Well, I am ecstatic. This one lucked out on giving me one wedding, so I get to plan your wedding." Mom chimes in. I grin, pulling back from Rhianna, knowing full well that it will be a nightmare for her.

"If you're planning it, you're paying for it. I

have a few non-negotiable requests," Rhianna says. Beckham and I are both shocked at her words. No way. Noah leans down to me as Mom and Rhianna start arguing about wedding decisions.

"She's doing it to give you two a break." His eyes flick to Beckham, who must have heard because he looks sad for a second before turning back to his game.

"We don't want her to do that," I say to him, to which he shrugs before walking over to our father who is trying to make coffee in the kitchen. I move to where Beckham is and sit next to him.

Nudging him with my shoulder, he doesn't look my way as I say, "Hand me a remote. I'm about to kick your ass." He does, and we play while they bicker. When our mother declares it's time to leave, she comes over to me and leans down and kisses my cheek.

"I'd like to see you this coming weekend. All of you, for dinner, please." I groan, and that makes Beckham smirk as he and our parents make their way out the door.

Looking to Rhianna, who sits happily on Noah's lap, I tell her, "Don't do that for us. We're fine."

"Hey, it's a win-win. We get a free wedding,

one that she was planning for you—and we both know Mom is great at wedding planning—and it occupies her time so she won't annoy you and Beckham."

Noah's phone rings and we both go silent to let him answer it. When he does, he flicks a quick glance at me.

"Give me a second, girls." Rhianna gets up, not even caring, but I know, I just know from that look that Noah just gave me, who is on the other end of that call.

"Ry, what's wrong?"

"It's August he's talking to."

"We don't know that."

I turn to face her. "Does he call often?"

"Yes, but..."

"It's him." We sit there and wait until Noah comes back. When he does, he asks, "What did I miss?"

"Was that August?"

"Yes," he answers.

"I need to go to bed." I turn away but peek back over my shoulder. "Has he mentioned anything about me?"

"No, sorry, Rylee."

When the days mix together, what is that called? I don't even know how long it's been since we lost Paige and August. A month? Maybe two?

I'd say two.

Beckham is back at school and frequently involved in fights, our mother is having a field day planning Rhianna's wedding, and me, well, I am taking it day by day, it's all I can do. Nothing exciting happens, just work, home, and then sleep.

Getting into my car, I think of what's in the middle console. Keys to his house, which I still haven't been to. I know I should go and get it over with, but I don't want to. I'm not sure I can do it.

I haven't called him again.

And I haven't asked Noah if he hears from him.

I drive to the local food market and get out. This was where I bought August food and he told me to leave him alone. This was where I wanted to follow him home from that day.

Going in, I check my phone for the list Rhianna sent me of items to grab for dinner when a hand touches my shoulder, making me squeal on the spot. When I get myself back under control, I notice a very pregnant girl stands in front of me.

"It's the right sister today, right? You're dressed differently," she says, smiling.

"What do you need?" I ask as her hand falls to her belly.

"I'm not stalking you, just so you know. It seems we shop at the same place. I saw you come in and wanted to say hello. I don't really know anyone, and no one wants to be friends with the girl who got pregnant by the guy who was engaged to one of the twin princesses," she says, looking me straight in the eye.

"We weren't engaged," I tell her.

"Okay, well, I think his parents want to take the baby from me. But that's not going to happen."

"Why are you telling me all this?" I ask her, not wanting to hang around and talk. I want to go home and dream—dream of *him*.

"Oh, sorry. I..." She looks behind her, and as she does, she pauses, and her gaze falls to the floor, making me feel bad. "Umm, so did you happen to drive here?" She raises her eyes back up to meet mine.

"Ahh, yes?" I say, confused.

"Well, my water just broke, and I was hoping you could take me to the hospital." She reaches for my arm and grips it tightly. "I have a fear of ambulances," she says, grinding her teeth.

I don't know what to say. I mean, should I do that? Then her nails dig into my arm, and I nod, putting my phone into my back pocket.

"Okay, let's go."

"Thank you. I'm sorry, this is probably the last thing you want to do. But I watched my mother die in an ambulance, and the last place I want to be is in the back of one of them." Her hands don't lose their grip as we start walking to my car. I unlock it, get her inside, and then run around to mine before I start the car and drive.

She moans next to me and pulls out her phone.

"I need to time them," she mutters to herself. "The midwife told me to time them." I assume she's referring to the contractions.

"What's your name?" I ask. I can't remember if she told me before because my mind has been everywhere.

"Jacinta."

"Do you want me to call anyone?"

"I have no one," she says sadly, and I feel bad for her.

"What about his parents? Do you want them there?"

"No. No way. They already want to take him from me." She moans then and drops her head. I try not to speed, but it's hard. Especially since she is having a baby right next to me. And no way in hell do I want to deliver a baby.

"What about Anderson?" I ask.

She takes a few deep breaths, then turns to me.

"Do you think I should?" She looks to me for guidance. Not really something I can give her. That is her decision, not mine.

"Maybe?" I voice it as a question for her to come to her own decision. She grabs her phone and opens to his number. After pressing call, she puts him on speaker.

"What?" he barks into the phone. *Asshole.*

"Hey, it's me."

"I know who it is," he says, not losing his attitude.

"Well, I'm on my way to the hospital..." She holds the phone out as another contraction hits her. I take it from her hand before she drops it.

"I don't have time to play this shit," he snaps.

"Anderson," I say into the phone.

"Rylee?" he asks, surprised.

"Yes. Jacinta is about to have *your* baby. Get to the hospital."

"Why are you with her?" he asks. "Will you be there?"

"Just get there and stop being a dick." I hang up on him and then put the phone down as we near the hospital.

"Thank you, I owe you," she says tiredly. "He's only coming now because he heard your voice."

"Good thing I won't be here, then," I answer as we come to a stop. I leave the car running in front of the emergency entrance and get out to help her. She clings to me as she leans out of the car.

"Thank you, Rylee, really. Thank you."

"Sure, no problem." I peer at the doors. "You'll be fine by yourself?" I ask her.

"I've lived most of my life by myself. Now I am anything but," she says, rubbing her belly as a wheelchair is brought out.

She's only eighteen and about to have her first baby all by herself because let's face it, Anderson doesn't do anything unless it serves him.

Jacinta waves to me as they wheel her in. I get back in my car, and as I start to pull away, I see his car pull in. He stops right next to me and stares. I look away. The last person I want to interact with is *him*.

Fuck Anderson.

Okay, well, I've done that serval times, and it sucked.

My sister calls as I drive off, probably

wondering where her food is. I don't answer. Instead, I drive to the one place I have been avoiding.

CHAPTER 8

Rylee

Sitting in the car, parked out the front of August's house, is a mental bitch.

Get out.

Don't get out.

Stay in the car.

Don't stay in the car.

The keys to his house sit in my hand, and the house stares back at me, closed with no one inside.

My phone starts ringing again. This time, I

answer it.

"Where are you?"

"I won't make dinner," I say and hang up on her.

My hands are sweating, and I don't know why. Nerves, maybe. It's not like he's in there. I know this. But it doesn't help the fact that every time I went into that house, it had to do with him.

I bet it even still smells like him.

Leaving my things in the car and only carrying the keys and my phone, I walk up to the front door. As I reach it, someone yells, gaining my attention.

"He's not in there, you know." I turn to find an older lady next door focused my way.

"I know," I say, turning away from her and unlocking the door.

"That's breaking and entering, kid," she shouts.

"I have a key," I yell back, not sparing her a glance as I enter. I close the door behind me and lean against it.

August.

It smells of August, just as I knew it would.

In the kitchen, I see my things neatly stacked on the counter. On top of the pile sits a white piece of paper. Reaching for it, I see his handwriting, which I might add is some of the nicest I have ever seen.

Rich girl,

Go to the bedroom, collect what is yours.

Take it. I made it for you.

No signature, but the demands are him. I know it. Scrunching up the note, I keep it in my hand as I walk up the stairs to his bedroom.

I keep my hands by my sides, careful not to touch anything because I'm afraid of the memories it may inflict on me.

Pushing open his door, I immediately see it.

My eyes fill with tears as I take it in.

He's made me my very own chest of drawers, and it's gorgeous. Flowers are carved into the front and sides, and on the top is carved 'Rich Girl.' No one, and I genuinely mean no one, has ever done something so thoughtful for me before.

My fingers lovingly skim over it, dipping into the delicate carvings. It's perfect, so perfect. I open the top drawer and inside is a picture.

It's one of him and me.

I don't ever remember taking one, but I know

when it was. Paige was here, and he and I were out the front arguing. We may have been fighting, but I'm looking at him the way I always looked at him.

With hope and adoration.

He is the most beautiful man I have ever seen.

Shutting the drawer, I drop to the floor, and the tears that I have been holding back seem to escape all over again.

Reaching for my phone, I pull up his number and press call.

He answers but doesn't speak.

"I just saw it..." I pause, turning back around to look at it and drag my hand over the wood. "It's beautiful. So beautiful, August."

He doesn't respond, but did I really expect him to? At least he is picking up when I call. I know it's him. Who else would answer his phone and not talk to me?

"I miss you," I whisper. And before I can say another word, I hang up and let the tears roll unchecked.

"Where have you been?" Rhianna asks, pacing back and forth when I walk in.

Noah sits down, watching her and shaking his

head.

"Where have you been?" she repeats as she stops her pacing and looks at me.

"I..."

Before I can even speak, she grabs hold of my hand and pulls me into the bathroom, shutting the door behind her.

"Look at that and tell me what it says."

"Rhianna," Noah says, his fist tapping on the door.

"Go away," she shouts, then looks back at me. I turn to where she's pointing and see a white stick.

Oh, fuck.

I take small steps until I reach it and peer down.

"It has..." I turn back to see her hands over her ears as she stares at me with eager eyes. I open the door so Noah can come in, and he goes straight to her.

"Guys..." both sets of eyes fall to me, "... you're pregnant," I tell them.

Rhianna shakes her head, and Noah looks to the floor, shocked. I stand there awkwardly, waiting for either of them to move or speak. Noah breaks first. He lifts Rhianna, wraps his arms around her body, hugging her tightly to him, and burying his face in her neck. I slide past them and out of the room to let them have their moment.

My sister is going to have a baby.

Holy shit.

It doesn't take them long to leave the bathroom, and when they do, I see Rhianna has been crying.

She wipes at her face and smiles. "I'm having a baby."

"Indeed, you are." I smile back at her.

"*We* are having a baby," Noah corrects her.

"Please. I'm the one who has to push her or him out. *I* am having the baby." Noah doesn't argue with her, just kisses her cheek again. She leans into him as she looks at me.

"Where were you?" she asks.

"Funny story—" Just then, someone bangs on our door. I turn and open the door to see Anderson standing there.

"Umm, hell no. You aren't allowed here," Rhianna says, but Anderson doesn't care. His focus stays on me.

"It's a boy," he says to me only. "Look, Rylee…" he starts, but I finish for him.

"No, don't say anything. You shouldn't be here."

"I love you, Rylee. I'll stop. I'll be good. Please, just forgive me."

"Nope, nope, not happening," Rhianna says, stepping up and trying to shut the door in his face, but his hand stops it, and he pushes it open a little to stare at me.

"Rylee, you know. You know we could be amazing together."

"You really are delusional, aren't you?" I say to him, shaking my head. His face loses that soft sorry look and instantly hardens.

"You think any other man would love you the same way I did?" he spits. "You couldn't even hold on to trash." He smirks.

"This is why you're single, asshole," I say, slamming the door. His yelp is heard as it hits on his fingers.

Rhianna laughs as Anderson pulls his hand away. When he does, I shut and lock it.

"Call the police," Noah says as we both turn to him. "You have a restraining order. Call the police."

"He just had a baby. That's where I was, driving Jacinta to the hospital," I tell Rhianna. "She's not all that bad, just fell for the wrong man."

"Haven't we all," Rhianna says with an eye-roll.

"Well, no. You didn't," Noah says, stepping up behind her.

"Ry." My eyes lock with Rhianna's at the serious tone of her voice. "Do you miss him?" she asks.

"Yes," I say with a sad smile.

"I think he misses you more," Noah chimes in, looking away. When he does, I narrow my eyes at him.

"What is it?" I ask him.

He leans down and puts his face in Rhianna's neck as if he's trying to avoid telling us.

She pulls away and turns to face him. "What aren't you saying?" she asks.

Noah scratches his cheek, then says, "He's here. For tonight only."

My heart rate picks up to a speed I'm not sure is right for me. "What?" I shriek in disbelief. How long has it been since I've seen him? Two months? I stopped counting after thirty days. It was too torturous for me to keep tally.

"Glenn needed his help, so he came back," he says with a shrug.

"Ry." Rhianna reaches out, and when she touches me, I see a soft smile on her face. "Think about it. Do you want to see him if he's only here for one night?"

Yes. The answer will always be yes.

"Noah, you should tell her where he is."

"He asked me not to."

"I'm asking you then. Where is he?" Rhianna asks, crossing her arms over her chest. He groans at her and checks his watch.

"He should be finished at Glenn's by now. He was staying at his place until he left again."

Again.

He planned to come in and then leave without so much as a word.

It's unfair, really. How can he feel that's okay, and it tears me to shreds to even think that? I could never do that to him.

Grabbing my keys, I leave everything else and go back to his place. He would have known I was there earlier since I rang him, and he answered. Why didn't he tell me to wait? I would have remained just to see him.

"Noah, walk her out." I only just hear Rhianna bark her command as I leave her and Noah behind me.

"Don't tell him I'm coming," I say as we get outside. Noah quickly surveys the area to make sure Anderson isn't here and nods.

"You weren't going to tell me, were you?" I ask him.

"No. It's unfair to both of you to keep seeing each other when you both know he should be gone," he says.

"That's not up to you to decide," I bite back.

"No. But think of the issues it will cause. Especially with Beckham."

Beckham.

He's only just started talking to me again, and losing him would kill me, as I'm sure it killed August to lose his sister. But August has no one. He's never had anyone his whole life to stand by him and let him know that he is loved.

Yes, I love him.

"He's only here for a night," I say back to Noah.

"Sometimes a night turns into longer," he says, thoughtfully. "Just be careful. You were hurt when he left the first time. Imagine how it will be a second time." He turns and walks back to the door but waits for me to get in the car and start it before he heads inside.

I shouldn't go.

I should stay home and crawl into bed and let him enter my dreams instead.

In them, we are safe.

In them, he doesn't break my heart and shatter it into a million pieces with just a few single words.

I should turn around.

But I won't.

I know I won't.

CHAPTER
9

August

Glenn is a mess, even if he resumes his day-to-day as if he is okay. He isn't. His house tells you so. He called me to help him clear out some of Paige's things. He couldn't do it by himself. He said he tried, and all that happened was he ended up seeing the bottom of a bottle.

I couldn't say no, even if I told myself I would never come back here. I had to.

"This is..." Glenn shakes his head and pours himself another drink. He offers me one, but I decline. "It won't get easier, you know. I still go to call her at night when she's pushing curfew. Then..." he trails off. I know what he means. "Anyway, thanks for the help. She really did love you."

"You raised her right, Glenn. You took her away from that place," I tell him, trying to give him comfort. I don't have much experience with comforting others, but the truth always works best for me.

"I should have taken you too. I knew how you were treated. Maybe if I did—"

"I'm fine. I'll always be fine," I tell him.

"You killed those men. I know you did."

I don't confirm it. There is no need for me to.

"And a part of me thanks you for that." He chugs his drink and pours himself another one.

"I should get going," I say, grabbing my helmet.

Glenn holds up something and offers it to me. "Take it. It was by her nightstand." I lean forward and take the small frame, and in it is a picture of Paige and me. I nod, not able to find the words of gratitude as I leave his house.

My phone rings, and it's Rylee. It's always her.

I sit down on the curb and listen to her sweet voice, which is like a melody to my ears.

I don't speak. It's better that way. She would just argue with me anyway. So, I listen. I listen to her tell me she finally found it and that she misses me. I itch to say it back. To tell her that I miss her too. But I don't because my demons are bigger than hers. My hands are covered in blood and could never again touch something so sweet. She hangs up, and I hang my head, wondering what life is going to bring me next.

Because it sure as shit has thrown a lot of punches my fucking way.

It's exactly as I left it. Not a thing has changed. I didn't plan to come back here. Maybe one day, but not this soon.

I did what I needed to do in this town, and it was best I left after that.

Shedding blood stains your soul. Watching the life drain from someone is a whole new level, though.

I don't regret my decision. I would do it all again in a heartbeat.

I smell her, though, my rich girl. I know she was here, and her scent lingers everywhere. That strong strawberry scent she gives off is lingering in my house. And I love it, even if I can't see her or touch her.

Headlights shine into the house through the front windows. I open the door to see a familiar car sitting in my driveway.

I know it's Rylee, even if I can't see her.

The car stays running, and she makes no move to get out.

Standing there, I wait for her to make the first move. I'm not sure how she knew I was here, but I can guess who told her. Even though I asked him not to. Noah's the only one who knew I was coming, and Glenn has been too lost in a bottle since I got here to call anyone.

Leaning against the house, I watch as she turns the car off, but her door stays shut.

I wait. It's all I can do.

A few minutes later, she gets out, and the breath is knocked out of me when she does. She's as beautiful as ever. Her dark eyes, which I have missed, lock on to mine as she keeps her distance.

I silently beg her to come closer.

It's her choice I tell my needy hands that want to touch her, grab her, and make her mine.

Rylee takes a tentative step closer to me, her heels digging into the grass as she comes closer. She's dressed in an all-black, tight-fitting dress. She hasn't gotten changed from work. Her hands, which are so familiar to me, reach up and touch her hair, pushing it back. Her eyes, the color of pain, search mine with need.

"August." I can hear the torment in her voice

as she speaks my name.

I don't respond, too afraid of what might leave my mouth if I do. Time hasn't changed us, it's too short. But distance can be a bitch. And even with every moment, every mile, I wished and hoped to just touch her one more time.

But if anyone knows anything, it's you don't always get what you want, especially when you're me.

"Do you plan to talk to me?" she asks.

I don't say anything.

How can I?

Words won't leave me, and I don't expect them to.

She huffs. "August." She says my name with anger now and takes a few steps closer, glaring up at me. "Say my name, August."

I refuse.

It won't happen.

That would be letting her in.

"August," she says once more.

Again, no words from me.

"Fuck you," she spits and turns, storming back to her car and getting in. I hear it start, but she doesn't put it in gear. She simply sits there looking at me.

I wait. Because I have nothing else better to do. And then she turns it off and gets back out. I watch as her whole body slumps.

"I love you, August."

CHAPTER
10

Rylee

I love him. I told him again. He needs to know he is loved.

So why isn't he moving, telling me he loves me too? He just stands there staring at me.

I want to punch him, slap him, tell him to speak. But I have a feeling he won't say a word. That's crossing a line for him, one he obviously doesn't want to cross.

Taking the steps two at a time until I am directly in front of him, his eyes never move from mine. They lock on, and I can see everything in him, know that, despite his hard exterior, he loves me as much as I love him.

He just has to remember.

He just has to admit it to himself.

Throwing my arms around him, I push up on him until my lips touch his. The weight of his lips on mine is like ice, cold and touchable, but you know if you touch it for too long it could cause serious injury.

August Trouble could cause me a severe injury, of that I am sure.

My lips move, and soon, he kisses me back, then his hands find their way around my hips, and he lifts me up, so my legs wrap around his waist.

He kisses me like our last goodbyes weren't enough.

That this one will be it.

He moves, and I am helpless to stop him and don't plan to as he walks us inside, kicking the door shut behind him as we go.

I feel him harden beneath me and know I won't be leaving anytime soon. He breaks the kiss, but I won't let go. I pull back to watch him watch me as if he's saving the vision of me to his memory bank.

I probably look like a mess, but the look he gives me makes me think otherwise.

I offer a small smile before I lean forward and kiss the side of his mouth with urgency.

He lays me down so my back hits the old couch, and he stands above me. I stay where I am and watch as he pulls off his shirt, followed by his boots. Then his hands fall to his belt, and he slips it through the belt loops.

He smirks when it's in his hands and pulls me up, moving my arms to my back while he kisses my neck, then he reaches behind me and ties my hands.

When he's done, he drops his dark jeans to the floor, and I get to take him all in.

The perfect curves of his face, to his rippled stomach, to the delicious V that leads to another part of his body that's currently standing at full attention.

August lets me soak him in before he turns and walks off. I hear the rattle of drawers before he comes back with a knife in his hand and he pushes me back on the couch. I should be scared, but with him, I never am. He leans forward, showing his teeth as he nips at my bottom lip, then pulls it between his own teeth, sucking before releasing and pulling back up. His hands fist my dress, and he pulls it away from my skin before the knife comes between my legs, and he starts cutting it from my body.

I don't stop him. I like the way his hungry eyes

eat me up as he cuts the fabric all the way up to my underwear. His eyes find mine as his hand skims the top of my panties teasing me with his touch. He leans down and blows hot air on my lace panties and then kisses me just there, my legs still closed, before he pulls back up and starts cutting again.

He drags the knife up, so it slices all the way past my stomach, rending the dress and exposing me to him. I have no bra on, as the dress was tight enough that I didn't need one.

August drops the knife to the floor, gets down on his knees in front of me, and starts dragging his fingers over my body, exploring me. I squirm, wanting him to touch me more, not tease me. When I begin to buck, he places his hand on my stomach and pushes me back down, shaking his head before he resumes his torture. When I start to move again, he grips my underwear and tears them away from my body, then drives my legs apart so he is between them, still kneeling on the floor, and pushes them open.

I feel the cold air hit me, followed by his mouth. He kisses me there before his mouth opens and his tongue dances with my clit.

I close my eyes and let him have me, my hands still tied behind my back as he inserts a finger pushing it in and flicking it inside me. His mouth never leaving my clit. I start moving my hips, and his other hand joins in, sliding between my ass cheeks so now he is in both areas. He looks up at me to make sure I am still okay before he resumes his sensual torture.

And boy does he. Soon, really fucking soon, after his mouth starts moving again, I come. My body shaking and my eyes closing as he makes me come with his hands and mouth.

Anderson could never do that.

I feel him back away from me, but I'm too high from the orgasm to stop him or even call for him to come back.

When I manage to open my eyes, he pulls me up gently, unties my hands, and sits next to me on the couch, his cock still hard. His hands fall to the back of the couch, and he sits there like a fucking king.

A very naked one at that.

I pull myself off the couch and look down at him. He still hasn't said a word to me, and I'm guessing he won't.

I put myself directly in front of him and crawl onto his lap. His hands remain hung over the couch as I pull myself up and over the top of his cock. He watches me, not what I'm doing, as I reach between us and position him.

"You've missed me, haven't you?" I ask, sliding down ever so slightly. I'm already wet and ready for him. "You've missed this." I take him all the way in. My head drops back, and that's when he reaches for me, his touch burning my skin. His hands slide up my back and wrap around my body as I start moving.

"I've missed you too, especially at night when I have to touch myself." He grunts but doesn't say anything.

My hands dig into his shoulders as I move faster. He lets me set the pace, riding him and satisfying my own hungry demands. I don't say anything else, because why should I be the only one talking?

It's unfair.

And I hate it.

I want to hear his rich voice telling me off, telling me I'm not right for him, but not stopping himself from touching me as well.

A phone rings in the background, but we both ignore it as I take my pleasure from him.

Just when I am about to come again, he smacks my ass hard, making me yelp in surprise and delight before I collapse onto his chest.

His hands stroke my hair, which was tied up but now cascades down my back. Gentle strokes, as if I'm all of a sudden precious to him.

I stay there listening to his heartbeat and wonder what kind of world it would be if I fell in love with him first. Then I close my eyes and sleep takes me.

I'm warm and not in my own bed. That's the first thing I realize when I wake up. As my dress was ruined, I'm still naked and lying on August's couch with a blanket covering me. I move and see he left me a shirt to replace my dress. Picking it up, I put it on and stand, looking around for him. That was the best night's sleep I've had in a long time. I head out back, thinking that's where he is—it's where he usually would be—but the garage is shut tight, and there is no sign of him. My phone starts ringing inside, and I walk in, finding it neatly stacked on the counter with my other things.

I pick up my phone to Rhianna's name flashing, more than likely to check up on me. I don't answer. Instead, I head upstairs to his empty room. All that's left in here is my dresser and his bed. No clothes are in any drawers and not a single thing of his remains.

I run down the stairs and out the front, looking for his bike, which I saw parked here last night, but it is also gone.

He left. Again.

And it hurts exactly the same.

Not even a goodbye this time. I manage my way back inside, and my phone rings again, but this time I answer it.

"You saw him, didn't you?" Her words ring through, and I start crying. Her voice grows softer as she says, "He left?"

"Yes," I confirm.

"Okay, well, that's okay. We survived last time. We can this time too," she says into the phone. "Ry, you *will* move on from this. You *will* move on from him."

"What if I don't want to? What if he was all I wanted?"

"Noah lost the love of his life, and he moved on, he loved again. Would you guess he loves me any less?" she asks.

No, not a hope in hell. He worships the ground she walks on.

"No."

"See? And he's a man, hunny. You are a strong woman. We birth children, raise men, you have more power than anyone. Come home, I'll cook pancakes with ice cream."

"Why does it still hurt?"

"Because love is pain, and pain is beauty. You'll rise from this and one day see the beauty in what you two had."

"I'll be there soon." I hang up the phone and press call on his number, but he doesn't answer this time. I press call again.

He *will* answer me.

He *better* answer me.

On the third ring, he picks up but doesn't speak.

"Don't you dare come back and do that again. You just left. Again. How could you?" I scream at him. I hear his breathing and the noise from his bike. "You hurt me more than Anderson ever could, do you know that? Don't come back, August. Don't you ever come back. I don't want to see you or breathe the same air as you again. Do you understand me?"

Again, no answer.

"Fuck you," I say and hang up.

He did that already.

Fuck me.

CHAPTER
11

August

"You're keeping a secret from her. What happens when she finds out?" Sully asks as he sits across from me. I haven't left town yet. But now, after that phone call, I know I need to.

"She'll hate me," I tell him.

"She may not." Sully shrugs.

"They have standards, and what I did would be disgusting to her, I know it." I scrub my hand down my face and shake my head.

"He hasn't told her yet, and I'm sure Josh told

him."

Josh, that fucking asshole.

"Speaking of Josh, you know your mother is back, right?"

I had heard, seen her briefly at the funeral those months ago. But because I haven't been back, I hadn't cared to find her. Why would I? She was never a mother to me.

"If Anderson hasn't said anything to her yet, why would he wait?"

"I don't know, but you should tell her."

"It's in the past. It's where it will be staying," I say, ending the conversation with him regarding that.

"Where do you plan to go?" he asks as I walk to the front door.

"I don't know. I've never left this city, so I guess wherever I end up."

"August." I turn back to him. "Are you sure you're doing the right thing?"

I look back to my bike.

Am I sure? I don't know. But I am.

"I'm like a leech in her life. If I don't leave, I will continue to suck all the light out of her."

"You're wrong. I see the way she watches you. She loves you."

"I have no doubt, and love makes people blind. They can never see clearly through their feelings," I tell him. "I have a wicked heart, and hers is anything but." Stepping out, I go to my bike and get on it. Sully stands at his door, watching me as I pull away. I drive past my house and see her car is no longer there. Glancing at the time, I know she would be on her way to work. She is never late. It's one of the things I like about her.

Driving to her work and parking off the street so she can't see me, I watch as she gets out of her car, locks it, then checks her reflection in the window.

There is no need. Nothing is out of place.

Everything is as it should be.

She straightens her shoulders as if she needs the boost. Maybe she does. I did leave her asleep, but she had to have known that was bound to happen.

I've told her before it could never work between us. Not once did words leave my mouth last night to give her any sort of false hope.

It's not something I am willing to give her, even if the lies sat on my tongue. They wanted to slither out and whisper sweet sorrows to her, tell her all her fantasies. So I bit it, hard, until it knew not to say a word.

It was the only way.

How do you make yourself stop loving someone?

It's next to impossible.

Her friend walks up behind her as she finishes checking her reflection and taps her on the shoulder. She smiles at her, and even through my helmet, I can tell it's forced.

Her friend bumps shoulders with her, and this time, she gives her a full smile—one I have missed so much—as they start walking to the building.

Getting back on my bike, I drive to Rylee's place. Noah's car is still there. When I get off the bike, he comes out to meet me, Rhianna standing back at the door, hard eyes assessing me.

"Sorry I wasn't in the office today. I've had things on." I nod. "She isn't here," he says.

"I know."

He nods and hands me the paperwork he's holding. I take it, thanking him.

"You're going for good?" Noah asks.

"Yep."

Rhianna comes over and slides her hand into Noah's.

"You can't keep on coming back. It hurts her a little more each time." I nod at Rhianna's words. "I want you to know you were good for her. You made her see her worth. So, thank you."

I've never really had anyone thank me for making another person feel before. Especially someone as precious as Rylee.

"I don't know if this interests you, but..." She looks up at Noah, then back to me. "Your mother lives down the road with a few other people if you wanted to say goodbye to her. We hear she's working now at one of the grocery stores and is doing well."

I take in her words and walk away. My mother is trying to be good. This, I must see. Driving to the closest store, I see her sitting out front, a cigarette between her fingers. She looks up and knows it's me. Her eyes go wide in surprise as she stands and walks over. I don't bother getting off my bike. Just lift the visor so I can see her better.

"You came to see me?" she asks, her brows raised high.

"I came to say goodbye," I tell her.

Mom's head drops, and a soft whoosh of air leaves her. "Will you come back?" she asks, hopefully.

"It's doubtful." I tell her the truth.

"I'm trying real hard. I want you to know that. And I will keep trying real hard."

"I hope you do."

"I even met a nice man. Real nice, August. He takes me for dinners and doesn't judge me."

"That's good. I'm happy for you."

She looks down to the ground. "I hope you're happy, despite everything."

I click the visor down, not bothering to answer her. That, she doesn't need to know. She has never cared my whole life, now she doesn't hold the privileged to do so.

She waves as I ride off.

I look back over my shoulder to see the town disappearing behind me.

Right where it's meant to be.

CHAPTER
12

Rylee

Five years later.

Rhianna steps over to me, her daughter clutching her hand as I walk out of work.

"Aunty." Summer throws herself at me, her little arms wrapping around my body. "I get to stay at your house tomorrow night." I nod and reach down to pick her up. She's getting big now, but I always have time for her cuddles.

"You do. What are we going to play tomorrow? Hide and seek?" I question her, raising my eyebrows.

"Yes, yes, let's." I put her down, kissing her cheek as Rhianna smiles.

"Mom has her tonight, and you tomorrow. Are you sure that's still okay?" she asks, checking. "I can always leave her with Mom for two, but Summer prefers to go to yours."

"It's fine. I only have plans tonight, not tomorrow." It's Friday, and it is not often I do make plans, but tonight, I have.

Rhianna rubs her large belly. They found out recently it's a boy. Noah couldn't be more excited. Rhianna, on the other hand, doesn't like being pregnant all that much.

"I need this. Oh, God..." She shakes her head. Noah is taking her away and letting her do whatever she wants. So that means massages and doing nothing. Rhianna owns the coffee shop now, so she's on her feet all day. Then running around after an almost five-year-old while pregnant, she definitely needs it. "Anyway, I just came to give you this." She hands me a bottle of wine. "A client gave it to Noah. It's expensive, and I don't want to see it lying around because it makes me want to drink it. So please drink it, so I don't have to look at it anymore." She turns her lips up into a smile.

I laugh and shake my head. "It could sit in your house without you drinking it if you hide it away."

"It could, but that's not fair." She shrugs and grabs her daughter's hand. "Anyway, have fun on your date tonight. I hope you get laid." She sings the last part.

"Mom, what's laid?"

I giggle at Summer's question and walk them to their car, which is right near mine.

"When someone lies down," she tells her, then looks over her head to me and rolls her eyes. "Give Winter kisses from me."

I nod, check the time and realize I need to pick her up.

My work has childcare situated right across the street and right next to the lot where I park my car. When I get there, I sign in and head to her room. I spot her straight away. Her dark hair matches mine, but when she turns around and spots me, it's her eyes that get me.

They're her father's eyes.

Forrest green.

She takes off running to me, and I let her fall into my arms and hold her tight as she wraps herself around me.

When Winter squeezes me tight, her little arms give me everything she has. I smile, the biggest of smiles that are made for just her.

"How was your day?" I ask, pulling back reluctantly. She shrugs her shoulders as I reach for her bag and start to leave.

How she can be so much like August without knowing him, I have no idea.

I tried finding him.

I tried calling him.

He cut contact with every person here four months after leaving, and I didn't find out I was pregnant early enough. I assumed it was depression, and I was just snacking too much. I didn't even get a belly until I was six months along.

Noah lost contact with him, Sully never heard from him, and Glenn couldn't find him.

We tried.

We all did.

I wanted him to know he has a daughter. Even if he didn't want me, he had a right to know he had Winter and to possibly get to know her.

Who wouldn't want to know her? She is beyond exceptional and my favorite person in the world. Even Rhianna would argue with her on who's my favorite, it's their favorite game to play but Winter always wins.

Walking back across the road to where I work, we go up in the elevator until we reach our floor. Winter tells me all about her day with such enthusiasm when we are away from everyone else, and I smile as I listen to her ramblings. When we get to my office, Winter lets go of my hand and runs from me straight to the big office at the end of the hall.

My brother.

Beckham stands from his chair and picks her up, swinging her around. She loves Beckham. To her, Beckham can do no wrong whatsoever.

Beckham is also my boss.

Yes, I never took over the business. I turned it down when Father offered it, but Beckham had already started by then. Now? Well, now, he has made the business even more profitable. He may not be as good as me with money, but, damn, he is good at business practices. No one can deny that.

Winter tucks her head in his shoulder as he sits with her on his lap. Beckham hasn't been in a relationship since Paige.

He's changed since her death.

I had heard stories about him, that he is rough in bed—which I did *not* need to know—and that he fucks them and leaves them.

He lets her crease his expensive suit and lets Winter mess up his perfectly coiffured hair. He may have hardened over the years, but he is a completely different person when he gets hold of Winter. Beckham's one of the most successful and youngest businessmen of the century. Because of that, he's been all over business articles, blogs, and social media. If he wanted to, he could have his pick of women. But he chooses not to.

"What do you plan to do for your birthday?" I ask. Beckham's turning twenty-three next week. See, still a baby.

"Nothing," he says, making Winter's bottom lip pout. "I'll hang with you, then." He loves Summer just as much as Winter—he is her uncle too, after all—but Winter and I, well, we don't have a Noah. All we have is Beckham.

"You sure you'll be okay with her tonight?" I ask him.

His eyes pin mine. "Yes, you know I am. We're going to have ice cream and watch *Frozen.*" Winter claps her hands at his words. I throw him my keys, and he hands me his.

"Don't hurt her, you know she's my baby."

I roll my eyes.

Beckham loves cars, and he prefers not to put a child seat in his unless it's essential.

I say my goodbyes, giving Winter a quick kiss on her head. She never seems to care if I leave when she's with Beckham. I love their relationship. It took a while for Beckham and me to get back to where we once were after Paige died, but now, we are even stronger.

Getting into his two-door sports car, I drive it back to my apartment. Rhianna moved in with Noah shortly after she got pregnant with Summer, and I took over the apartment. I even bought it from my parents. They refused to take the money, but I worked out a way to pay them so they couldn't refuse—I took the money and bought my mother a car.

When I get home, I go straight for a shower, washing off my day.

Tonight is my first real date in years. I tried to date when Winter was one, and of course, none of them went great. Let's face it, small children are hard work and I was always tired back then. So I decided it was best I didn't date. My life now revolves around Winter, and that's how it should be.

On the other hand, Rhianna had other plans, and now, here I am, sliding on a little pink dress, followed by some matching heels, to go on a date with one of Noah's friends whom I've met only a hand full of times, knows I'm a single mother, and still wants to take me out to eat. Go figure!

I pull my hair from the bun it was in and run my fingers through it before I pin half of it back up, then apply some light makeup.

"You can do this," I say, giving myself a little pep talk.

Oh, gosh, maybe I can't. I sit on my bed and

take a few deep, centering breaths.

Do I really want to date?

I still compare everyone to August. Even after all these years. Even when I know, I shouldn't. He could be in another country, or dead, for all I know, and yet I still do it.

I hate that I let myself down like this. Really, I do. But I can't hate him. I could never hate him. Even if I tried.

Pulling myself up, I leave the house before I chicken out.

Holden is nice. He opens doors for me, pays for my food, and buys me drinks. I sit opposite him at the bar after dinner. I don't have to be home tonight so I'm taking full advantage of my time away from Winter and trying to be myself for a little while.

"I've told you already you look good, right?" he asks, his eyes moving from my face to my legs. He has, multiple times and I like the attention. I haven't had this type of attention for a long time.

Holden leans in closer, so our lips are almost touching. "We could go back to mine. I have much better wine."

I don't want to say no. Holden is good looking. Nice. And it's not the first time I have met him.

But it's our first date. So should I?

Rhianna said I shouldn't, but she is also getting sex.

I, on the other hand, am not. And I could really do with a male appraisal of my body. Preferably with his hands and mouth.

I nod, and Holden smirks, waves his hand for the check, and places his hand on my thigh.

I get giddy by that simple movement. It doesn't help that we've had three glasses of wine at the bar and two more at dinner.

"Do you have to work tomorrow?" I ask, leaning into him as well. He turns to me, his lips pulling into soft, thin lines before he answers, "No, I'm all yours."

He also knows I have a kid, which is reassuring because my body isn't the same as it used to be. I have white lines on my thighs, and my boobs don't sit as high as they used to. They need more support now—no more perky boobs after you have a child.

The waiter comes over, and Holden pays, stands, and takes my hand in his to help me up before we start walking out.

I pause when we get to his car.

Should I?

"Rylee," he says. It's a stark contrast to what Anderson would call me. Baby. He would scream it. It was disgusting.

"Sorry, just stuck in my head."

He nods as if he understands. Holden is a few years older than me. Why he isn't married? I don't know and haven't cared to ask.

Should I ask?

I'm not sure.

He dresses well, isn't a felon, has a job, and is polite—tick, tick, tick, and tick.

So why isn't my heart beating out of my chest for him?

"Let's get out of our heads. I know all too well what that can do to you."

"What?"

"Being stuck in your head. It's what I do. I'm always stuck in my own."

I smile at his nice words as he opens the car door for me, and I slide in. I watch as he strides around to his side of the car, then he drives to his place.

I'm about to have sex.

Holy shit!

CHAPTER
13

Rylee

His house is lovely, but I didn't expect it to be any less if I am honest. Compared to my apartment, this place is a mansion. It's on the fourth floor of a building, and he has the whole floor.

It screams money.

And I am very much used to money.

He shows me around, lingering at his bedroom, leaving the door open as we walk back to the wine area. Yes, I said that. He has an extensive wine area. He opens the wine cabinet and reaches for a bottle.

"This one is my favorite. You must try it." Holden pours us both a glass. His sleeves are rolled up on his blue button-up shirt, showcasing his forearms. He has nice arms. He smiles at me, his sun-kissed hair perfectly in place.

I take my time, letting my eyes take him in, much the same as he did to me.

"Would you prefer I remove the shirt?" he asks, lifting one brow, obviously catching me in the act. He hands me my glass and I lift it to my lips.

"Yes, very much so," I reply with a smirk.

He doesn't waste any time, putting his glass down and unbuttoning his shirt, one by one, before he slides it open and off.

And I look.

Oh, boy, do I look.

My Jimmy Bob in my drawer just isn't doing it for me like he should be. I need friction, action, hands roaming my body, a mouth touching me. I *need*.

Standing, I walk around to him, the glass still in hand as I come to a stop in front of him.

"You're not what I imagined," he says, reaching for my face.

I lean up to look him in the eyes, noticing they look like chocolate, as I wait for him to speak again. "You're oh so much better."

I reach for his stomach, my fingers dancing on his bare skin. His abs fit and not what I pictured most lawyers to be. Though Noah is an exception.

"Do you want to finish your wine first?" he asks, sliding my hair back and reaching for me. His hands touch my neck and slip down the back of my dress, so I finish the wine quickly and place the glass down, then close the distance between us. He takes it, letting me, and unzips me from the back.

I let my dress fall to the floor, leaving me in nothing underneath. I kind of hoped I would be getting lucky tonight. I'm glad that it's coming true because lately, I have been stressed.

"Should we take this to the bedroom?" Holden asks, pulling back slightly so he can read me. I nod and turn around. I can feel his eyes burning into my ass as I saunter to his room.

Hands catch me before I hit the doorway, and he taps me on my ass before I feel him come up behind me.

"You are something different," he whispers and turns me around. He's gentle with me, but I want him to be rough. I want to feel his hands sliding all over my body firmly and forcing my lips apart as he kisses them. Instead, he leans in to kiss me, his hands now falling to my hips, one finding its way between my legs. His kiss is soft.

I've been kissed many times in my life. I've had sloppy kissers, hard kissers, and soft but gentle kissers. But the only one who has managed to kiss me the way I like is August.

And I hate that he has ruined me for all others.

No matter how hard I try not to, I hate that I compare every single man who touches my body to *him*.

It's unfair, really, because Holden seems like a good guy. A decent man. Someone I would like to date. Someone I could potentially fall for. Maybe.

We both drop onto the bed, and he is careful not to put all his weight on me. His mouth doesn't stop as he keeps kissing me, his hands now on either side of my hips, abandoning between my legs.

I pull away between kisses, and he pulls back too. He lifts off me, takes off his trousers, and puts on a condom before he falls back onto me.

He's a decent size, and I'm excited, nervous. All the emotions are running through me simultaneously as I feel him position himself between my legs. He looks down at me, and I smile up at him.

He goes to speak, but it's not the words I need right now. It's movement. I need to feel. I lean up, my lips touching his as I pull him down, so his body is entirely on top of me, and I buck him with my hips, letting him know to move and that I need him there.

When he finally does, he stops kissing me, but our lips are still touching, and I am the only one doing all the kissing.

He makes a weird noise when he is fully seated inside me. It's something between a grunt and a scream. I pull my lips away to see his eyes closed, and his mouth is open in the shape of an O.

"Arghhh," leaves his mouth, and he opens his eyes to look down at me. "That was..."

I stare at him, confused.

Did he just finish?

No. No way.

He only just...

"Do you need me to finish you off?" he asks.

Oh. My. God. He did finish.

What the ever-loving fuck?

"I'll be fine," I tell him.

That's a complete lie.

"It's been a while since ... you know." I feel

sorry when he says the words as he pulls out of me and lies next to me, disposing of the condom.

"Oh, sorry, me too. How long?"

"A month," he says before his hands run down his face.

A month.

What the fuck?

I sit up and try not to shake my head.

"I may get going. I have to do a few things for work."

"You sure I can't make you stay?" His hand settles on my back, I turn to look at him. "Just for a little while longer?" he asks. I look down to see his cock becoming hard again.

"Only if I'm on top," I say because I really want to get fucked. He smirks, reaches over and grabs another condom, putting it on, then lies back.

I move so I can climb on top of him, and before I do, I reach for his cock and give it a light stroke. He makes that O shape again with his mouth as I climb up higher and position myself over him.

"You're so hot."

Hot? That shit makes him sound like a teenager, but I take it anyway.

Sliding down on him, he starts to make those

grunting sounds, so I take the lead, hoping to get something out of this for me, as it seems he already has. His cock is a decent size, and I start sliding, moving my hips back and forth. He brings his closed fist to his mouth and bites on it, but I don't stop my friction. I need it. Oh boy, do I need it. I reach down for his hands and place them on my breasts. I also need contact. I want contact. He grabs them but doesn't make any move to do anything with them. When I glance down, I see his eyes are closed, and he's lost in concentration.

My body doesn't stop moving, even when I feel he's almost there. It wants to reach that state of pure bliss. It's been so long since I've reached it with a man and not a toy—it's just not the same.

"Argghhh." There he goes again.

Fuck.

Shit on a damn duck.

My hips stop, and I fall off him. I didn't even get halfway there. This totally blows. I get off the bed and walk out to find my dress. After slipping it back on, I grab my purse.

"You leaving?" he calls, not bothering to get up.

"Yep," I yell back with a shake of my head.

"I want to see you again," he says.

"Ummm..." I look toward the door and pull out my phone, messaging for a cab. "We will see."

He walks out, naked, and leans on the wall.

What's with the cocky look?

He really shouldn't be after that performance.

Holden has a great body but is *terrible* in the bedroom. At least if he knows that fact, he should try to make the women come first. Gosh, it wouldn't hurt him to eat some pussy, would it?

"I really like you, Rylee." My shoulders slump as a message from the cab company comes through, telling me it will be a few minutes.

"I'm not looking for anything now, okay?" I tell him with a smile. "Have a good night, Holden." I walk out, closing the door behind me.

I don't want to live a life of making my own orgasms. That would suck.

A lot.

I want a man to at least try and make me come before he takes his pleasure.

Honestly, he makes Anderson look like a king in bed.

I call Rhianna. It's late, but she can't sleep lately with how far along she is.

"Shouldn't you be in someone's bed right now?" she asks as soon as she answers. I look back to his building as I speak to her. "That's a negative, thank you very much."

"Oh no, is he an asshole? I swear he's always nice to us."

"No, he isn't. But—"

"But what?"

"Rhi, it literally takes him thirty seconds and he comes," I tell her quietly in case anyone can hear me.

She starts laughing. Hard. I stand there and wait for her to finish as my cab arrives and with a sigh, I get in it.

"Are you done yet?" I ask her, now I am on the way back to my apartment.

"Hold on." She keeps laughing and eventually, her laughter dies down. "Okay, I'm done."

"Bitch," I say into the phone.

"Don't you know it." She starts laughing again. "But seriously, give him a chance. It can't all be about the sex."

"It's a big part of it," I reply.

"Okay, well, maybe he can improve."

"Nope, not happening." I end that conversation right there and now.

"You just compare everyone to..." She doesn't say his name. "Anyway, you should stop that."

"Easier said than done."

"Go home and play with your Jimmy Bob. I'm sure he'll know how to get you off."

"He does. And he does an outstanding job all by himself." I smile. "But I'm tired, so I'm gonna go and pass out."

"Good. Beckham doing okay with Winter?" she asks. "I don't know why you let him babysit. It's funny, really."

"They love each other, and she has fun with him."

"Yeah, but he's out every night doing God knows what."

"Not when he has Winter," I tell her, smiling. Our mother says the same thing, but Winter idolizes Beckham, and I love their bond. It's unique and something I will always protect, no matter what the cost.

"I know, he loves her the most," she says.

"I love you the most," I reply.

"I know. Okay, enough of my jealousy. I know it's because of her," she says, meaning Paige. Winter does look a little like Paige. But that's not all of it. When I had freak-out moments when she was little, I couldn't call Rhianna because she had a baby as well. It wouldn't have been fair. So I called Beckham. And he always came. He will always come because he is my brother, and we love each other.

"I'm almost home. Can I get Beckham to pick Summer up on the way before he drops off Winter?" I ask.

"Which car does he have?" she questions, knowing his love for cars as well as we all do.

"Mine."

"Yes. Can do."

"Rhianna."

"Yeah?"

"Leave him alone about women." She chuckles then we hang up. She always gives him shit about his harem of women. One time she walked into his apartment, and he had two women naked on the couch.

Well, needless to say, he will never live that down.

CHAPTER
14

Rylee

I ended up going home and trusting Jimmy Bob to finish the job Holden could not. Bob never lets me down. Apart from that one time when his battery died. That was awful. Bob left me hanging on a cliff I just couldn't fall over, even with my fingers.

I sit at the café as I watch the two girls run in and out of the play area. Rhianna is due back today after I had Summer the night before. Holden tried messaging me. He even tried calling the next day, but I declined both attempts. I'm not sure what to say to him. So, it's better left unsaid.

My phone dings. It's Rhianna telling me she's ten minutes away. I peek at the girls and see them tapping each other on the head as they try to play Duck, Duck, Goose but fail.

Someone laughs, and I turn my head just as the door to the café opens. I watch as Sully walks in, followed by someone who makes my heart stop.

Dead. I'm dead.

My eyes are wide, my body has frozen as I watch August walk straight to the counter dressed in dark jeans and a yellow shirt. He has a light stubble on his chin, his hands are tucked into his jeans as he looks at the menu.

August is here.

He isn't dead.

I assumed he was, but he appears perfectly fine. Better than fine, actually.

He looks good. Too good.

Asshole.

"No, no, no, no." Summer comes running out and pulls my hand. I wrench my gaze away from him and to face her. "Winter won't share with me. Tell her to share." I glance up at August again and see him staring at me with wide eyes.

Yeah, I know how that feels, buddy.

Fuck you.

It's been five years. And here he is, looking like he stepped out of a magazine. His eyes flick to Summer, then back to me.

Something looks different in that gaze.

"Go get Winter. We have to leave," I tell Summer, looking away from him. Summer pouts at me but does as I say. I stand, gathering all their things, not even caring that I only just ordered my drink. I have a need, to get out of here. Cleanse my eyes. Do something.

"Rich girl." His voice sounds as good as I remember.

Summer runs back out, clasps her hand in mine, and smiles at August. He looks at her, then at me. "She looks like you."

"It's because my mummy is her twin, silly." I see the air whoosh out of his chest as he nods, then he looks to me and smirks. He smirks—the asshole.

"We need to leave."

"Mummy." Winter runs out and slams into my legs. August's gaze moves down to her. I watch him for a reaction seeing if he notices it. Because I do. Every time I look at her, I see him. Winter snuggles into my leg, and August drops down to a crouching position so he is eye level with Winter.

"And what is your name?"

She looks up at me, and I nod, giving her permission to speak. She smiles when she answers him, "Winter." He glances up at me. "Paige," she finishes, proud of herself for remembering her middle name.

"We have to go." I pull my bag up over my shoulder and leave the food and drinks.

"Rylee." His use of my real name almost slays me. I laugh. It's fake and forced and a little crazy.

"Rylee," I repeat my name while shaking my head. "Goodbye, August. Maybe in another five years, we'll see each other again." I grab both the girls' hands and walk off.

"Goodbye, Winter," he says. She turns around and smiles at August, offering him a small wave. I walk to the car and call Rhianna, who answers straight away.

"I just left the café, we can't meet there. Abort," I say and hang up. Getting the girls in the car, I shut their door, and when I turn around, he's standing there.

"You had a kid," he says, those eyes I stare at every day in the face of my daughter stare back at me. "And she looks like me."

Heart meet floor.

I push past him and get into my car. He

doesn't stop me, just stares as I pull out and drive off.

My hands shake and my eyes want to cry, but I keep it in. I can't let it out. No way in hell can I go back there.

Driving to my place, I pull up to see Rhianna and Noah already waiting for me. They must have been close to arrive before I did. I get out of the car, turn around and see both the girls asleep in the back.

"August was there. He saw Winter," I tell them, almost blurting it out. My hands are shaking, and I have to remember to breathe. Rhianna covers her mouth with her hands, and her eyes go wide. Noah shakes his head like he can't believe what I've just said.

"He's here? You're sure?" Noah asks.

"Very much so," I tell him.

The sound of a loud engine comes up behind us, and we all turn to see a Harley Davidson pull in behind my car. I watch as August gets off. He removes his helmet and licks his lips, that small scar that used to be there barely visible now.

"Noah." August nods to him.

"Rhianna." She swears and holds her belly.

"I'll take the girls inside," Noah says, then proceeds to open the car to get the girls out while Rhianna steps close to me so her arm rubs against mine as she gives August the best death stare.

"You shouldn't be here. Why are you here?" Rhianna asks him.

"Sully's mother died," he says. Then his eyes move to me. "I didn't expect to see you."

"You had hoped to not see me," I tell him. "We can always pretend you didn't."

"No can do, rich girl."

Winter groans when Noah grabs her and August's eyes fly to her.

"I think we should talk."

I start laughing. It's something I do now instead of going crazy. Rhianna steps back, and August glues his eyes to me.

"Talk," I say calmly. "Talk. I tried talking to you, calling you, finding you. Nada," I scream. "So, no, we *will not* talk right now because you deem it to be. Fuck off! I have to get my daughter ready for bed."

"Our daughter, right?" he snaps back at me. I look him over and see the glint of a ring on his finger, not just any finger either—*the* finger.

"You're married," I say. The incredulous sound in my voice makes the last word sound like a screech. "Go away, August. Just go away." I turn and walk to my apartment, where it's safe and where my daughter is currently located.

"Oh, don't you even think about following. I will kick you so hard in the dick, you'll be seeing stars." I hear Rhianna say as I walk inside.

Noah walks out, nodding to me as he goes and gets Summer. I grab my phone and call Beckham straight away.

"This better be urgent." I hear the laughter of a girl in the background.

"August is here." I hear shuffling, followed by the jangle of keys.

"I'll be there in five." He hangs up, and I lie back on my couch, exhaling deeply. I wait until I hear the roar of the engine again as it leaves, and Rhianna walks in with Noah and Summer.

"So, I would ask how your day is going but—"

"Probably not the wisest thing to ask," I say.

Rhianna laughs and kicks my feet so I can make room for her pregnant ass on the couch.

"Holy shit, Ry. Holy shit. First, you have the worst sex."

"Oi," Noah says, which makes Rhianna giggle.

"She did." She shrugs in my defense. "Then, you see the only man you've ever wanted with a ring on his finger." She sighs. "Fuck! I used to complain my life was hard."

The door to the apartment opens and Beckham walks in and looks around.

"He left," I tell him.

Beckham walks past us and opens Winter's door before he shuts it quietly and walks over to me. "I'll kill him," he says.

"No, he's her father," I say reluctantly.

"A father isn't just a sperm donor, Ry. And that man is not a father."

"He never had the chance to be." I'm not even sure why I am defending him.

"Well, I guess we'll see what he does with this information, then," he says, crossing his arms over his chest.

"Eww, you smell of cheap perfume." Rhianna gags, motioning to Beckham.

"It's because before you called me, I was balls deep in a blonde." He smirks, making Rhianna scrunch up her nose at his words before she hits him. "What was that for?" he asks her before he starts rubbing his arm.

"Because you are a manwhore. Stop it already."

"Maybe when I'm in my forties," he replies with a wink.

Rhianna rolls her eyes right back at him and shakes her head.

"Ry, are you okay?" My hands are shaking as my leg bounces up and down on the spot.

"I think so."

"It's August. You know him," Noah says.

I shake my head. "I thought I knew him, but I most certainly don't."

"We don't have to worry about it now. Get some sleep. Beckham will stay and watch Winter, right?" Rhianna says, grabbing her belly. "And maybe Summer, too," she adds through gritted teeth.

"Umm ... you're peeing yourself," Beckham says as we all look to Rhianna, who is standing with her hands on her belly as she tries to stay upright.

"Yeah, I thought they would go away when we got here. Seems they haven't."

"Fucking hell," Noah says, handing a bag to Beckham, then reaching for his wife's hand before he rushes her out of the apartment.

"I can always get a hit put out on his head. I'm sure a lot of people would do that for free. August has a *lot* of enemies."

He does—a lot. Or did...

Anderson is one of them. Anderson only ended up serving a small amount of time for what he did to me, and I keep my distance from him, trying not to see him. He had a child with Jacinta, who I heard left with the baby not long after giving birth.

I don't blame her.

His family has been trying to track her down all this time with no luck. I didn't know her for long, and she seemed to be dealt a shit hand, but I hope she's doing okay. The thing is, she seemed nice, and she most certainly didn't deserve to be stuck with Anderson.

"He's her father. No matter what happened between us, it will only hurt Winter in the long run," I tell Beckham.

He nods and flicks the television on.

Both girls are asleep in Winter's room, and I leave Beckham to his own devices as I head for my bedroom. My phone lights up with an unknown number as I sit on the edge of my bed.

Can we meet tomorrow, just you and me?

I know who it's from without even having to check.

On my lunch break. Meet me at the café
across the street at 12.

He replies with a thumbs up as I lie down on my bed.

August Trouble is back in town, and I'm not sure how I feel about that.

This could go either incredibly bad or worse.

CHAPTER 15

Rylee

I'm tired, have been most of the day, and Shandy keeps pointing it out as well.

"You know you look like shit."

I roll my eyes at her. She's become one of my closest friends over the years, and I'm tremendously thankful for her. Not sure what I would do without her.

"Thanks," I reply sarcastically, then apply some lip gloss.

"Do you really need that?" she asks, walking

over and touching my hips, pulling my dress down, and smoothing it out with her hands.

"Yes, I do. He has to know what a dick he is. And while I tell him, I want to look my absolute best."

"You want to look better than his wife," she states with a grin, but I know she's right. "Should I go and tell Beckham?" She wiggles her eyebrows, knowing full well if he knew where I was going for lunch he would follow. Beckham and Shandy are also great friends, which is rare for Beckham, considering most women he knows, he fucks and leaves. But Beckham has the wrong body parts for Shandy, and I don't think Shandy's girlfriend would like it. At all.

"Don't you dare. If he needs me, tell him I'm out for lunch." She rolls her eyes and hands me my purse.

"I would say good luck, but I'm not sure you need it. Maybe he does from you, though." Her eyes roam me as she assesses my outfit.

"Do I look okay?" I ask while walking toward the door.

"You look great. Just remember, you raised that child. He ran away, and *you* did everything to find him."

I nod. I know I did. I even hired a private investigator who came up with nothing. Sully knew I was looking for him, but I didn't want to tell him why. I thought that should be something I needed to tell August in person, but I never got the chance to. I always thought I would find August, but my extensive search never turned up any results. Not even a solitary lead as to where he was located.

"Okay, I got this."

"You do," she says with an encouraging smile.

I don't, but fuck me, I have to.

Leaving the building and walking across to the café, I see him before he sees me. His head is down, his foot is hooked up on the wall, and he's staring at his phone as his fingers move fast over the screen—such a difference to the man who hardly ever used his phone when I knew him. I step over to August without him noticing and finally stand in front of him. When he realizes I'm there, his eyes roam me from bottom to top before they stop on my eyes.

"Thank you," he says.

I nod, and he steps away, holding the door open for me to head inside first. I do so, knowing full well he is directly behind me every step of the way. My hands sweat as I pull out a seat and he sits directly opposite me.

"I honestly didn't think I would see you again." August leans back in his chair. He has light stubble on his face, and I wonder what it feels like.

"I assumed the same thing," I reply.

"She's mine, right?" he asks, getting straight to the point.

"She is," I tell him honestly.

"Wow! Umm, okay ... that answer has taken me a little by surprise, but also not if you know what I mean." I'm surprised by how he's talking to me. He's changed—a lot. "Does she know about me?"

I nod in response.

"Would she like to meet me?" he asks.

Again, I just nod.

"Fuck, rich girl, we had a kid."

Again, another nod. It's all I can give him right now. My mind is working overtime because my eyes keep falling to the ring on his hand.

My phone starts ringing on the table and I look to see Holden's name flash across it. Silencing it, I glance back up at him to see him watching me.

"You've hardly changed. You still look—"

"You've changed. Are you married?" I ask, nodding to his hand. "You have to tell me, August. I can't have strangers in my daughter's life."

"Yes, I am."

Head, meet gun.

Boom.

Wowser.

While I regain my composure, I think about how much I struggled to move on when he did it so easily. It's unfair when I think about it.

"Is she here?" I ask, trying to keep my voice neutral.

"No, she's back home." Wow. Umm, okay. "She won't meet her until you're comfortable," he says.

"Sure." I nod.

We sit there, in an awkward silence, both of us simply staring at each other.

"I think if we just keep this about Winter, we should be able to do this," I say as my phone lights up and Holden's name pops on my screen once again.

"I think that man is trying to reach you."

I nod, reaching for my phone. "Holden," I answer. "Can I call you back? I'm busy right now."

"Yes, okay, can do. I just wanted to see if you would meet me for dinner this week."

"'I...'" August is watching me, so continue with, "...would love to. Let me call you back later, okay?"

"Your boyfriend?" he asks.

"I don't know." I stand, tucking my phone in my bag. "I get home around five, bathe Winter, and we have dinner. If you want, come over after that. We can take it slow and see how she does." I don't give him a chance to respond as I turn and walk out of there as fast as possible. I run across the street, and as soon as I am in my building, I walk to the bathroom, close the door, and sit on the toilet as tears stream from my eyes.

I had hoped if he ever came back, it would be for me.

I was wrong.

So wrong.

"We have a visitor coming over today. Are you excited?" I ask Winter as she gets dressed in her pajamas.

The doorbell rings, and she smiles big. "Can I get it?"

I nod and follow her out of the room to the door. When she pulls it open, August stands there dressed in jeans and a nice white shirt that hugs his body. He looks good, almost better than he did five years ago. How is that even fair?

"Hello, Winter, I brought you something," he

says to her, holding out a small bouquet of flowers.

She takes them and runs back to me. "Look, Mom, look ... flowers like you get from Holden." I nod, smiling, and when I look up at August, his eyes are flint hard. I can't quite work out that look, and I'm not sure I want to either. I guess it's none of my business now.

"Why don't you come in? I just ordered us some dinner. Hope you still eat Indian. It's Winter's favorite," I tell him as he steps inside and shuts the door behind him.

"Yes, I do."

"Good, have a seat."

Winter sits at the table, and August sits next to her as I bring out plates and drinks. I get a message that the food has arrived and go retrieve it. When I turn back, I see Winter pointing at her room, telling August which one is hers.

I only pause for a second before I walk over and start serving her food, then mine, finally handing the rest to August. When he takes it, our fingers brush, and I pull back as if it didn't affect me.

It did.

Of course, it did

Winter starts telling him all about her day.

She says it with such happiness that I even get lost in the conversation. She does have that effect on people.

"And you go there all the time?" August asks, referring to her daycare.

"Yes. Next year she starts big school, don't you, baby?" I say, smiling at her.

"I'll be at the same school as Summer," she says excitedly. Winter turns to me and looks at my phone. "He hasn't called yet." She sticks her bottom lip out in a pout, so I pick my phone up and dial my brother's number, handing the phone to Winter. She jumps from the table and runs to her room with the phone in hand.

"Who's she calling?"

"Beckham," I tell him, and he nods, seeming to be more relaxed with those words.

"Are they close?" he asks, looking toward her room. We can see her sitting on her bed, holding her toy and telling Beckham all about it.

"The closest. No one could separate them."

"Much like you two are." I think on that for a second and then nod my head, knowing how close Beckham and I am. He's my brother, and our affinity for each other will never be broken.

"Beckham is the only father figure she's had. I love their bond."

August's eyes go hard at my words, then he

squints and shakes his head. "He isn't her father."

"Of course, he isn't. He's my brother ... her uncle. And, really, the only person I trust implicitly with her."

Winter comes running out of the room and hands me the phone, I take it and stand, saying hello.

"Do I need to come over?" he asks.

"No, it's all good. Have a good night, okay?"

"Okay, I'll see you tomorrow." Beckham hangs up before I can say anything else.

"Uncle Beckham is going to take me swimming this weekend."

"Is he?" I ask her, wiggling my brows. She curls up on my lap, with her head on my chest.

"Summer said that he is my daddy. Is that true, Mommy?" she asks, peering up at me with sleepy eyes.

"Who, darling?" I ask, and her little fingers point to August. He just looks at me for confirmation. "We can talk about this another time, okay?" I reply.

"I've never had a daddy before," she says on a yawn.

"Would you like August to put you to bed?" I ask.

She simply nods, and August stands and looks down at her.

"Just pick her up. She gets really lethargic when she's tired."

He does as I say, taking her from my arms, and walks with her to her bedroom. I sit there and listen as she asks him to read her a book. His voice is soft, the cadence slow yet eager. I can't do it any longer. I can't sit here and listen to him with my daughter. I start cleaning the table and washing the dishes.

As I finish the last one holding it in my hand, August comes out, rubbing the back of his head.

"You've done well with her. She's perfect."

"I know," I say, smiling. Don't all mothers think that about their children? I know I do.

"I want to be mad at you, but I can't. Not when I was the one who left." My hand grips the clean plate. I am unable to move. "I'm moving back," he announces.

"Where?"

"I never sold my grandmother's house. It's still there."

"Oh," I reply. I have avoided that place for a long time.

"Will your wife be coming with you?"

"Her name is Mary, and yes, she will."

"Winter has to get to know you before she gets to know anyone else," I tell him with a firm voice.

"I know. I would never do anything like that unless I cleared it with you first. You are her mother."

I nod at his words. "Thank you."

"Thank you for raising her. I..." He pauses. "She is perfect. She's the perfect mix of us."

"She is, but she has your eyes," I tell him.

"It would be a crime for anyone other than you to have yours," he states as he walks to the door. I'm not sure how to respond to those words, so I stay in the kitchen as he passes to the door. "Goodnight, Rylee."

He says my name.

My name, not rich girl.

A tear leaves my eye, and I let it fall.

It's the end of an era.

And I am helpless to stop it, or my heart from beating in my chest.

I think it may have broken a little bit more.

CHAPTER 16

Rylee

"So you're saying I don't get her this weekend?" Beckham asks as he walks into my office.

"No, she has to get to know him."

He shakes his head and walks out.

I start to pack up the rest of my stuff and get ready to leave when Shandy walks in.

"Your sister out of the hospital today?"

"Yep, I'm about to drop Winter off for a play date with August while I go visit her."

"Are you okay?"

I pull my bag up my arm and nod. "It's going to be weird for a while. I'm so used to not sharing her."

"Well, you have Holden to keep you company." She laughs.

"Shut up! I agreed to see him again. Not sure why." I blow out a heavy breath.

"Because despite his bedroom antics, he is a good guy. Maybe focus on that." She pauses. "He only really needs to be good with his tongue." She pokes hers out and wiggles it.

I laugh at her antics because I can't help it.

"Okay, I'm going now. Stop it." I shake my head at her.

"If you say so. Don't go falling in love again."

Yeah, that cannot happen. But at the same time, I wonder if I ever truly fell out of love with August.

"That's a pretty big house," Winter says as we come to a stop out the front. August is already on the porch waiting. It's been two days since I last saw August. Now, I'm getting Winter out of the car to have a sleepover with him, at her request. She likes him. Let's face it, I don't blame her.

"Do you think I will get my own room?" she asks.

"Maybe," I tell her. Grabbing her bag, she runs, letting go of my hand and going straight to August. I turn just in time to see him pick her up and her little hands wrap around his shoulders.

Walking over, he puts her on his hip as he reaches for the bag in my hand.

"Should we show you and Mommy your room?" he asks.

Who is this man? And what on earth has he done with the August I knew?

"You made her a room?" I ask.

"Yeah, just built some things and bought a few things. The rest she can pick."

I nod. Not entirely sure what to say to that. I follow him in and come face-to-face with a house that has haunted me for a long time.

It looks much the same, but now it's more welcoming. He's purchased a new television, and it's on, not like it ever was before. I stare at it, shocked to see even that small change.

"Yeah, I figured she would like TV, so I went and got one of those Apple TVs everyone talks about," he says, answering my unasked question. "She likes Disney, right?"

"Yes," I reply, just as she starts singing a song from *Frozen*. I smile at her as we walk up the stairs past his bedroom to one a little farther down the hall. The door is open. The walls are painted pink, and there are Disney princess decals on the walls. From the ceiling hangs a few snowflakes and other cute things. There is also a carved chest with toys and some books. But then I see the pièce de resistance and ask, "You made the bed?" Stepping into the room to take a closer look, there are snowflakes carved into the headboard. It is beautiful and perfect for a little girl.

"Yeah, do you like it?" he asks Winter but looks at me. She claps her hands in excitement, and he puts her down.

"Mary didn't want to come here, but she's arriving in a week. Just so you know."

I nod at this new information.

"You plan to introduce them?" I ask.

August reaches up and scratches the back of his head as he looks at me. "Would that be okay with you?"

Uncomfortable—that's what this conversation makes me—totally uncomfortable.

"I would like to meet her first, before you bring her around Winter," I reply. Not just because I would like to see who August fell in love with, but because Winter is my most precious thing in this world.

"I would never bring anyone around her who

would be bad for her."

"I know." And I do. He was the same with Paige. Protective. "I should get going. I have a date I need to get ready for." I drop to my knees and call Winter. She comes running into my arms and almost knocks me over.

"August said ice cream after dinner, Mom. Ice cream," she says excitedly.

"Not too much. You know how it makes your tummy sore," I remind her, standing and kissing her cheek. She runs back to the toys in the chest that has the same carved snowflakes as the bed, checking out the few dolls that wait inside.

I walk out, and I hear August's soft steps behind me.

"You have a date?" he asks.

My hand is on the railing, ready to walk down to leave, but I turn to look back at him as he stands at the top of the stairs.

"I do."

"You've been seeing him a while?"

"Yes. Well, no. But I have known him for a while. He works with Noah," I tell him.

"So, he's a lawyer?"

"Yep."

"Must make your mother very proud," he bites back at me.

"I'm not sure. How about you tell me what your wife does?"

"She's a mother. That's what she does," he says, fighting back.

"You have another kid?" I ask, shocked.

Holy fuck! Why didn't I think to ask that?

I take a step backward and almost miss the step, but regain my footing and shake my head.

"No, she does."

"Okay." I spin around and walk out.

He doesn't follow.

Did he ever?

Holden is, well, Holden. I didn't have time to visit my sister before the date, and even though I offered to cancel it, she insisted I go and come later, as that's bub's sleeping time. She had a healthy, beautiful boy. Noah is over the moon to not be surrounded by so many women.

"Are you sure I can't persuade you to come back to mine tonight?" he asks, reaching for my hips and bringing me forward so our bodies are touching.

I place my hand on his chest as I look up at him. "I can't, sorry."

Holden leans down, his nose rubbing mine. "Such a pity." His lips touch mine as we stand in front of my car. I drove myself tonight, knowing I wasn't going to go home with him.

I let him kiss me. His kisses aren't bad, but they aren't mind-blowing either. His hands find their way to my ass, and he squeezes it, pushing me against him, and I feel his hardness on my stomach.

My phone starts ringing, and I go to reach for it, breaking our kiss, but he doesn't stop. His kisses keep coming on either side of my face and down my neck. His body is still glued to mine, making it hard for me to pull my phone out.

"Hello."

"Just come back to mine. We can visit them in the morning," Holden says.

"Rylee." August's voice comes through the phone. It's so weird to hear him say my name. I'm not sure I will ever get used to it.

I push Holden off and step back from his mouth. "What is it? Is Winter okay?" I ask, my voice rising.

"She asked for you. She was a little upset, so I told her we would call you." August's voice is annoyed, not with Winter, but the bite in his voice is directed at me.

"I'll call back in five minutes. Let me get to my car."

"Mom, can you come here? Please?" Winter's voice sounds teary in the background.

"She wants her mother," he says.

"I'm coming." I hang up, look at Holden and smile. "I have to go. Thanks for dinner, Holden."

Holden's smile drops and he nods. "Call me later this week?" he asks.

I nod and climb into my car and drive straight to August's. When I arrive, I get out of the car and head straight to the door and softly knock. I hear August's voice telling me to come in, and when I do I find him on the couch with Winter curled up on his lap, asleep.

"She fell asleep?" I ask, glancing down at her as I step in a little closer to them.

"She did." I notice his forest green gaze tracing my outfit. It's a short, red dress that I matched with some black heels, and it makes my cleavage look amazing.

"Is she okay?" I ask, leaning down and kissing her cheek, which in turn puts me close to him. So close that I can smell him. Everywhere. I suck in a breath and pull away, knowing full well he is married, and I would never be the person to break that up. Not ever.

"Yes, she's fine. You can leave if you like."

"I have to get to Rhianna's anyway. Are you sure you don't want me to take her?" He looks down at her sleeping form, and when he talks next, he doesn't meet my eyes until the last word leaves his lips. "She sleeps exactly like you."

"I should go," I say, straightening and making my way to the door. When I look back, August is still in the same spot with her cradled in his arms.

"She's quite literally perfect. How was she when she was a baby?" he asks.

I answer from my spot at the door, not daring to go near him again. "She was a great sleeper, as long as she slept next to me. She was breastfed until she was six months, and I went back to work. She isn't a fussy eater, and she loves almost everyone she meets."

"So, she's perfect," he says.

"I like to think she is ... yes."

"I'm sorry, Rylee. I'm sorry for leaving. If I knew..." He looks over his shoulder to where I stand at the door.

I shake my head at him. "It was meant to be this way. I had you for a moment, so I could have her for a lifetime," I tell him, then walk out the door, shutting it gently behind me. I get in the car and sit there for a moment, looking at his house and wondering if it could have worked if he'd stayed.

Probably not, but the thought is nice.

CHAPTER 17

August

I never thought I would be a father. It was never something I dreamed about being. Considering I never had one, I wasn't sure of the right way to go about raising a child since I never had a good example. But when I saw her, I knew without a shadow of a doubt she was mine. It was like something inside of me clicked, and I needed her. I wanted to be in her life, no matter the cost. And believe me, there is a cost.

"Mommy is here," Winter says, jumping from the table when her mother knocks on the front door. Winter opens the door and flies straight into Rylee's arms. I love them together. In the small amount of time I've seen them together, I know their love is unbreakable. It's a love Rylee has always deserved, and I couldn't give to her, but some part of me did.

"Hey, sorry, I'm early." She pushes back her dark hair and steps in. She's in shorts that showcase her long, toned legs and a shirt that falls just above her belly. She looks good. Then again, when doesn't she?

"It's no issue. I was hoping you would be. Mary is on her way. You're welcome to stay..."

"No, I think I may get going. We have a barbecue today at my mother's." Winter runs up the stairs and comes back down with her bag in hand, and Rylee places her hand on her hip as she looks toward me in the kitchen.

"I cooked her pancakes..." He pauses. "She asked."

Rylee chuckles and the sound rings through my body.

"Yes. Nutella and ice cream as well," she confirms as Winter nods and runs over. Her little arms hug me then she begs me to pick her up. I do, and when she's on my hip, both her hands come to my face. "You want to come to Gramma's?" she asks.

I see Rylee flinch at the question.

"No, not today. I have some people coming over later." Her bottom lip pokes out at my words. "But maybe I can stop by later and bring you and Mommy dinner. If Mommy is okay with that?"

"You'll have company," Rylee says.

"They can stay here. I'd like to spend as much time with Winter as possible."

She studies the floor for a moment, taps her foot, and brings her gaze back to me. "That should be fine," she says reluctantly, then looks at Winter. "Come on, Summer is probably waiting for you."

I carry Winter out, following Rylee to her car. She opens her car door, so I can put Winter inside. I kiss her cheek, then shut the door.

"Thanks," I state, being thankful for the time Rylee is giving me with our daughter.

"It's not a problem," she replies, then reaches for her own door. I reach out, stopping her from opening it and look at her.

"I want to talk to you about having her more often."

She blinks at my words, then shakes her head. "That's a little fast. Can you not just accept what I am giving right now?" she asks.

I let go of her hand and shake my head. "I've missed so much."

"That is *not* my fault. If you would have come back..." she bites back at me but trails off as well.

"I couldn't. If I did, I would have destroyed you." I tell her the truth.

"You wouldn't have. I'm stronger than you think, August. I've survived a lot while you've been gone. You getting married, and God knows what else ... I've survived."

My fingers want to reach out and caress her face, grip it and hold it between my hands and tell her she is still the most beautiful thing I have ever seen, but I can't.

"It was your choices that sent you away, and now it's my choice to decide about Winter. She may be part of you, but she is all me, August. All. Fucking. Me. And I would slit your throat before I let you take her from me. Do you fucking understand?" Her teeth grind the last words out.

She's hot, so fucking hot when she's angry.

"I understand." Her jaw loosens. "But that doesn't mean I have to listen. I'll see you tonight, Rylee," I say, stepping back.

"August." I wave and keep walking. "August, don't be a dick."

I chuckle at her words until I get to the house and open the door. When I turn around, I see her getting in the car and pulling away.

"This is..." Mary looks around, her eyes going wide as she does. "It's beautiful, August. It really is." She pauses when she gets to Winter's room. "You made her a bed?" Shock is evident in her tone. "You haven't done that in a long time," she says with an uneven voice. "It's beautiful, as I am sure she is."

"She is. Winter has my eyes."

Mary smiles, but it doesn't reach her eyes. Her son runs up the stairs and straight into Winter's room. He's older than Winter, not by much, but looks so much like Mary.

"Come on, Oliver, you have your own room, too." I open another door down the hallway and show him his bedroom. It's not much, but what she sent over I set up, so he had a place of his own. Oliver is a good kid. Quiet and shy but good.

Mary stands next to me, her hip touching mine. "I don't know if this is the right thing to do," she voices her concern.

"It is, I'm sure of it," I tell her.

She looks at me, her brows pulled together. And before she can say anything else, I walk off.

CHAPTER 18

Rylee

He's true to his word, showing up for dinner with food in his hands. He brought Winter's favorite, butter chicken. He walks in after I open the door for him and places it on the table.

"Is she here?" he asks, looking around.

I nod to her bedroom door, but before I can call her, Winter comes running out and straight into his arms. I feel on some level she knows exactly who he is because she has never taken to anyone the way she's taken to him.

I go into the kitchen, getting plates out, as she

starts telling him about her day and what she did. He glances at me every now and then but listens to everything she has to say with intent and never interrupting her.

I watch, wondering how different it could have been if he was here, raising her with me instead of running.

But that's not a healthy thought to have.

Could we have stayed in love?

Would our love be invincible?

I feel it would have been.

"Mommy." At her voice, I turn. Food is served and they are eating. "Can Auggie stay the night?"

I smirk at her name for him because I once called him the same thing. "Do you want to stay?"

"If it's okay with you, maybe on the couch."

Winter claps her hands. "We can have popcorn and watch movies and fall asleep on the couch." I laugh because I know she will fall asleep straight after dinner. She falls into a food coma every single night.

"Sounds like a plan."

"I'll leave as soon as I wake," he says.

I stand, pushing my chair back, and look at him. "I'm going to have a shower. Can you make sure she brushes her teeth before you start a movie?" I ask. He nods, and I walk off into my room, shutting the door. Sliding down it, I listen to their voices talk on the other side of the door.

I can't keep her from him, not that I would choose to. But that also means he will be back in my life, and not in any way that I always thought he would be.

"Auggie." I hear her giggle at him, and I smile. As long as she is happy, I am happy.

I am.

I really am.

If I say it enough, maybe it will etch into my brain.

Standing, I jump into the shower and quickly wash, then get out. Tying my hair back and throwing on my nightgown, I step out to find them both on the couch, Winter's eyes closed, snug in his arms. I go through and tidy up quietly before I switch all the lights off and turn the television down for them to sleep.

"Rylee."

I turn to see August watching me. "Yes?" I ask, my heart rate picking up.

His eyes drink me in from top to bottom and then he shakes his head. "Never mind." His hair is a mess, and he is fully clothed as Winter sleeps peacefully next to him.

"She has asked about you," I tell him. "I told

her you would be back, and one day she could meet you."

"And what if I never came back?" he asks.

I shrug. "I would have let her find you in her own time." I turn and head back to my room. "Goodnight, August." I shut my bedroom door behind me and crawl into bed, pulling the covers up over my face and silently scream into them.

August left as soon as I was up the next morning. Beckham came around not long after and wanted to spend a few hours with Winter while I did my grocery shopping. I couldn't say no. He's been missing her, and by the way her arms constricted around him, I would say it's been the same for her. I watch as they go off to get ice cream while I walk into the grocery store. As I grab a few things, I look up to see someone I haven't seen in a long time. Walking over to her, she doesn't notice me until I am standing next to her.

"Jacinta?" I ask. She turns, her face full of fear until she sees it's me. "How are you? I haven't seen you since I took you to the hospital. I heard you had a healthy baby, congrats."

"Yes, Oliver. He's just wonderful."

I smile at her. "I have a daughter now. Are you visiting or just passing through?"

Her eyes skirt around. "I moved back."

"Oh, good, that's great news."

"Look..." She pauses. "You have no idea who I am, do you?"

"Umm, what do you mean?" I ask, clearly confused.

"I changed my name a while back, so he couldn't find me," she says, referring to Anderson. "I'm Mary." Her face remains carefully blank.

I look at her, confusion creasing my brows until it clicks.

August.

Mary.

I flick my eyes to her hand to see the ring sitting on it. A band that matches his.

"Um..."

"I'm sorry. I assumed he was going to tell you."

I step back, putting some distance between us. "Look, I have to go." I put my basket full of my food on the floor and turn to walk out. I hear her call my name and have a déjà vu moment.

Haven't we been down this road before?

As soon as I'm out of the store, I pull my phone from my pocket and call him.

August picks up after the second ring.

"Mary..." I say with a shake of my head, "... is Jacinta. Really, August?" I pause, then scream, *"Really!"* I hang up and sit in my car as I watch Beckham walk over with a pleased Winter in his arms and an ice cream I know she won't finish. My phone starts buzzing, but I don't answer, knowing it's him.

"What's wrong?" Beckham asks, getting in once Winter is buckled in.

"Let's just go home," I say and put on a smile for Winter.

Beckham stares at me the whole drive, knowing full well something is up. When we arrive at my apartment, Winter yells from the back, "Auggie." We turn to see him standing with his arms crossed over his chest as he watches us.

Beckham gets out first, opens the door for Winter, and picks her up in his arms.

August walks over and nods to Beckham. "You've grown," August says.

I don't hear what Beckham says back as they shut the door. I stay in the car, not wanting to get out, not wanting to listen to his voice. I jump when Beckham's knuckles rap on the window. He nods to the apartment and walks off with Winter in his arms.

The passenger door opens, and August climbs in and shuts the door. His phone starts ringing and he pulls it out. "It's Mary," he says.

"Don't you mean Jacinta?"

"No, Mary. She left Jacinta behind a long time ago."

I huff and wait for him to talk, but I don't think I can look at him right now.

"She was upset that I had started building again." My body relaxes at his words. "The last thing I made was the dresser for you, which, I might add, you left in my room."

I did exactly that because I didn't want the reminder of what I had lost.

The man who didn't love me enough to stay.

"I've been working odd jobs, enough to always pay the bills, and I had plenty saved from when I did work here all those years ago," he continues. I feel his stare on me. "It wasn't Winter who I made it for. It was all for you. You used to watch me, and you believed in me when no one else would. I made it all for you, Rylee."

"I think you should stop talking now and go back to your wife." My voice doesn't break when I speak, but it's close, though. However, somehow, I hold it together.

"She's a good woman, I'm sure you know that. She had to hide from them. You know how dangerous he can be." I shiver at that memory. "It started off as a way to help her, then it led..."

"To more," I finish. I finally turn to him, holding everything back. "I'm happy for you, August. I really am. I'm glad you gave someone a chance. That you didn't hide and try to stop it like you did with me. I get it now. I get that I wasn't enough for you, that you and I were just a moment in time and were never meant to work." I take a deep breath and force a smile. "I'm happy for you," I repeat again. "Now ... please ... get the fuck out of my car and go home to your wife. I'll call you and we can co-parent. We don't need to interact anymore other than when it's about Winter. I won't keep her from you. She loves you already, and she deserves a father." I take a deep breath.

Green eyes lock on to mine.

"How come you haven't married?" he asks. "I always thought you would. I had nightmares of you so in love with your new husband."

"I had Winter. She is my life."

"If I had known—" he says.

"It is the way it is."

His phone starts ringing again, so he presses accept, and I hear Jacinta's, I mean, Mary's voice chime through. "I saw Rylee today." I hear her say, and his eyes find mine.

"I know," he replies.

"You know?" she asks. "You're with her, aren't you?"

"I am," he answers. "I was just leaving. I'll be home in ten." He ends the call, lowers his head, then raises his eyes back to me. "I have to go."

I wave my hand to the door. "As I said, you should go." I force a smile.

"Rylee..."

"Leave, August. You and I don't need to talk unless it's about Winter."

"You don't want to speak to me?" he asks, his forehead scrunching like he does not understand where I am coming from.

"No, I really don't."

August pushes open the door, and I watch him get out. Just before he shuts the door, he leans down, staring into my eyes. "If I had a choice, Rylee, it would've been you. It's always been you." He shuts the door and walks to his car.

I hold back everything until I see him drive off.

The tears fall, and they keep falling even when Beckham walks out, pulls me out of the car, and wraps his brotherly arms around me, making me feel safe.

"It's better this way," he says quietly. I nod into his chest, knowing he's right. "Just keep saying that and one day you may believe it."

I chuckle through my tears then pull back and look up at him.

"When are you gonna get your heart broken? Don't you know pain is beauty?" I say to him, avoiding all talk of his heartache from Paige.

"Girl, I'm fucking fabulous. This face is pretty enough. No need to get it broken." His face is strained with a forced smile, but you can see the lie behind his eyes.

"If you say so."

"I do. And so do all the girls who suck my cock."

"Eww." I shake my head as we walk back inside to find Winter at the table with her iPad. "You could have one like her," I say and nudge him with my shoulder.

"Nope, she is enough for me, thank you very much. My sperm do not swim for anyone."

"You're a manwhore, you know that, right?"

He smiles proudly. "I just can't keep the ladies off me. What can I say?"

"How about 'no'?"

"I only like to use that word in the office." And he's right, all the staff are scared of him. Beckham is a powerhouse in the office.

I often wonder, though, where he would have gone, who else he might have been if Paige was still here. I have a feeling we would have a lot nicer Beckham than what we have.

CHAPTER
19

August

Mary is sitting on the front porch when I get back, a drink in one hand and a cigarette in the other. She hardly smokes. But when she does, it's either because she's stressed or drinking.

Which is both right now.

She eyes me as I make my way up the steps.

"It's always been her. Even for Anderson, it was always her. Though I am not comparing you two, it was the same." She blows out a heavy breath and picks up her glass, putting it to her lips.

I can't offer her words of comfort because she's right.

It has always been Rylee.

It will probably *always be* Rylee.

"I don't think I can do that again." She puts the glass to her lips and drinks.

A car pulls into the driveway, and we both turn and watch as a familiar figure slides out. Blond hair and dressed in a suit, he walks toward us, his angry eyes falling to me before they land on Mary. "Jacinta," he says, his tone not to be messed with.

"It's Mary now, Anderson."

He nods, then steps closer, but not close enough that I can touch him. "You've been hiding. You've done well keeping my kid from me," he spits.

"Do you blame me?" Mary says back to him, hardly fazed by him at all.

Anderson grinds his teeth in response.

"I mean, you did try to rape a girl in the woods, did you not? And you expect me to just what? Let you come near our son?" She laughs heavily, throwing her head back. "You really are fucked up, aren't you? Did you have a fucked-up childhood to make you this way? Or does it come naturally?"

"You shouldn't have come back," Anderson

says to her, then looks at me. "You shouldn't have come back either."

"And what ... do you plan to make me leave?" I ask, crossing my arms over my chest. "The last person who did that..." I leave that hanging in the air, and he takes a step back.

"I know who you are, August. I know what you did." He bites his lip.

"I know what I did too, and I'm not ashamed of it either. Are you?" His fists bunch up at his sides and Mary steps in front of me.

"Maybe it's best we speak in a public area." Her hand comes into contact with mine, she weaves our fingers together, and he doesn't miss it.

"Why are you here together?"

"August is my husband," Mary says proudly. She wasn't so proud moments ago.

I watch as the news registers on Anderson's face. It's like watching a horror movie. First, his brows bunch up in confusion, then it slowly moves to a sly smile.

"You didn't come back for her?" he asks. "Even though she had your kid." He smirks. "I guess she wasn't worth it for you after all." I go to take two steps toward him to knock some real sense into him when Mary tugs at my arm, pulling me back.

"You should leave," Mary says.

"Yeah, maybe I should. Even go and pay Rylee a visit. Would that be okay, August?"

"Leave," Mary says louder, her nails now digging into my hand as she holds me in place.

He salutes me as he walks backward. "I'll be seeing you all." He looks back to the house then to Mary and asks, "What did you name him?"

"Oliver. His name is Oliver," she tells him, but I don't know why.

Anderson walks to his car and gets in, and we watch as he drives off. When I turn around, Mary reaches up and kisses me. She tastes like bourbon and cigarettes.

Her hands circle around my neck, and she pushes her body into mine, her lips almost bruising me. She doesn't stop, not even when I don't kiss her back, not even when my hands push her away. She stays where she is, her lips on mine until she can no longer keep them there, then her head comes to lay on my chest.

"Do you think you ever could have loved me?" she asks.

I lift her chin and look into her sad eyes. "I do love you," I tell her truthfully.

"I know you do, but you have never been *in love* with me. Have you, August?"

I pause, not sure what to say to that.

"I get it. You had Rylee first. She is your great love. But I just thought, with time, it might have changed to me." A tear leaves her eye, and she wipes it off before it can fall. "I'm not sure if it's wise I stay here." Mary steps back, putting some distance between us.

"Don't. Oliver is comfortable here. Stay."

Her head starts shaking. "See, you can't even deny it. Right then would have been your opportunity to deny it, August." She turns, walking back inside the house, leaving me standing there wondering what I could have done differently.

CHAPTER 20

Rylee

I always try to stay away from my parents' parties because they are a bore. Quite literally. But I promised I would go to one, and Mother has requested this one be the one I attend. My dress is a blush pink that fits perfectly over my body and drapes all the way down until the back touches the floor. It's loose over my breasts but tight at my waist. My hair is up with loose braids, and my makeup is flawless, thanks to Shandy, who is a six with the brushes.

"So pretty." Winter comes in and gently runs

her hands over my dress.

I smile down at her. "No, you are. Look at your Elsa dress. You're a true ice princess." She twirls in her blue dress as the doorbell rings. "You excited to spend some time with August again?" I ask. She only nods as I reach for her hand and walk to the door. When I open it, August's eyes flick to mine, then to what I am wearing.

"You look breath-taking." His voice doesn't waver, and his eyes are heated.

"See, Mommy. You're pretty."

"But you are our princess, right?" I lean down and kiss her cheek, careful not to smudge my nude lipstick. "Isn't she a princess, August?" I ask him, standing again.

"She sure is."

"Will she be at yours tonight ... or?"

"Yeah, if that's okay. I can always get a hotel if you aren't—"

"It's fine. I don't know Jacinta well, but she isn't bad." I add, "I hope," more in a whisper but I know August hears.

"She isn't," he confirms. The glint of his wedding ring makes my eyes fall to it again before I quickly glance away.

Winter reaches for August and pulls on his shirt for her to be picked up.

"Oh, sorry." August turns with Winter in his arms as Holden walks up behind him.

Holden nods to him, offers him a smile until his eyes catch on me, then he steps past and reaches for me, his hand coming to my hip and pulling me to him before his lips touch my cheek. "Beautiful."

"See, Mom, so pretty." I nod to Winter and look past Holden to August, who is staring daggers at Holden.

"Hi, you must be the new nanny?" Holden offers his hand, but August looks at it with disgust and doesn't take it.

August's eyes lift and flick to me. "I'll be going now." He turns and walks off with Winter.

"I'll be back. I have to give Winter her bag," I tell Holden.

He nods and walks to the table and takes a seat, pulling out his phone. I run out the door to catch them. August already has her in the car. He goes to open his door but stops when he sees me.

"Her bag," I tell August, handing it to him.

"That's your man?" he asks.

I wrap my arms around my middle. "We're seeing each other," I tell him. That's as much as I say because that's all there is right now.

"He's a lawyer. I bet that made your parents real happy."

"They don't know. Well, not until tonight anyway."

His brows go up in surprise. "You plan to introduce him tonight?" he asks. I nod. "Well, that's a big step." He looks down to Winter. "I have to go."

"Thanks again, August. And sorry about him saying you were a nanny. I haven't told Holden yet who you are."

"But you plan to, right?"

"Tonight." I say the word, but I'm not sure I believe it.

"Goodnight, rich girl." He smirks as he gets in the car, and butterflies take flight in my stomach at those two little words.

I watch as they drive away, and when I turn around, Holden is already waiting out the front for me.

"Noah called. He's already there wondering where we are." He reaches for me and pulls me in and kisses the side of my neck. "We could always stay and keep them guessing."

"No, it's okay. I promised I would be there. Are you good to go?" I ask, pulling back. "I just need to grab my purse." I run inside and grab it. Holden is already in his car waiting when I return.

And my mind is still thinking about how those

two little words left August's mouth.

Rich girl.

Who knew such small words would make my belly want to fly away?

Holden doesn't do that for me.

But August is married.

And having dreams of him is not appropriate.

My mother is the first to greet us. She always opens the door at parties to make sure who comes in is invited. Her eyes flick to Holden, then to me. She is pleased.

It makes me hate it a little more.

My father comes up behind Mom and reaches for me, kissing me on the cheek, then he shakes Holden's hand. Holden introduces himself, and when he does, his hand goes around my hip. I focus on him and his perfect good looks, and I wonder why when his hand touches me, I don't get excited.

What is wrong with me?

"Come, let's have a drink." Holden gives me a squeeze as we walk in farther, then goes with my father while I stand near the door with my mother.

"He seems lovely."

"August is back," I tell her, smiling.

Mom's face drops and a look of dread crosses over it. "That's okay, we can get Noah to handle him. He won't ever see her. You have nothing to worry about." She taps me on the shoulder.

"He has her right now." The words leave my mouth with intent. Mom has always made it clear she never liked August. Why so much hate for him, I will never know. She even begged me to leave his name off Winter's birth certificate. That I could not do.

Her hand reaches for mine, and she pulls me to the side room where there are no people and raises her brows at me. "Have you lost your goddamn mind?" she lightly screams. And yes, I said lightly. She has that down pat. Mom knows when to raise her voice and when not to. It's all about image.

"No. She loves him," I inform her.

"Winter loves love, we all know that."

"This is her second sleepover, and she is over the moon," I go on.

"You just..." My mother's head shakes, and she puckers her shiny red lips. "It's really unacceptable, Rylee. Do you even know who this man is anymore?"

"He's married."

"That's good. At least I know he won't be

coming around you again," she says in triumph.

"Yes, Mother." I walk off and find my sister sitting down, holding her baby, as people walk around her. I reach out my hands, and she places him in my arms, and I take the seat next to her. "I told her," I tell Rhianna.

"Huh?"

"I told Mother that August is back and with Winter now."

Rhianna tries to fight the smile that touches her lips but is unable to do so. "Tell me, did her right eye twitch? It has been lately, every time I tell her something outrageous. I swear I'm just telling her shit now to annoy her."

I laugh and gaze down to a sleeping Benjamin. He's so peaceful.

"No, it didn't." When I look back to Rhianna, her eyes have softened, and she lays her hand on my arm. "Are you okay?"

"I will be."

"It's okay to still love him, you know. No one is saying you have to stop."

"Apart from the world. He's married. Married to the woman who had Anderson's kid, of all people," I say quietly.

Rhianna's mouth hangs open and she shakes her head in disbelief. But before she can speak again, two people stop in front of us. Rhianna straightens and turns to face them while I hold the baby in my arms. Both sets of eyes fall to him and then on me.

"We missed all this. It makes me regret so much," Anderson's mother says. I don't even know why she's here. Her son is never invited back into this house again, but I guess my mother couldn't say no to them.

"Maybe if you raised your son right..." Rhianna snaps at them with a noticeably big, broad smile. Cold eyes the same as Anderson's glare at my sister. Anderson's father does nothing but gaze off into space.

"You should mind your tongue," Anderson's mother says to Rhianna.

Oh shit! I cringe, knowing full well she won't take that.

"Me?" She starts to chuckle, then stands. "I mean ... you've met your attempted rapist, no-brain, shithead, dick full of ass son, right?" She looks around. "We aren't in crazy town right now, are we? You do know you raised spawn? The best thing for that child is to stay away from you, so he has a good chance of being normal."

"I can see why you aren't the favorite," is all she says in replies, then her eyes flick to me.

"It was good seeing you again, Rylee." I watch as they disappear into the crowd.

Rhianna stands in front of me pacing back

and forth. "If I didn't have milk leaking from my tits right now, I would smack that bitch."

"I wouldn't object." My phone starts ringing, and Rhianna reaches for it and answers for me. I look down at the baby, not even paying attention to what she's saying when she hands me the phone back with no one on the line. "Who was that?"

"August."

"Umm, okay. Why was August calling?"

"Winter said she put her binky in your purse." Rhianna grabs my purse, opens it, and finds Winter's little pink stuffed mouse toy. She sleeps with it, loves it, and has trouble staying asleep without it. "He's coming to get it." Rhianna rubs her hands together. "This is going to be so good."

"Rhianna."

She turns to me innocently. "What?" She smiles. "Mom can't say no to Winter, so it will be interesting how she does when she's with August."

"My daughter shouldn't be involved in any of this." I stand, lifting the baby with me. As I turn, I see the door open and my mother standing there with a sour expression on her face before she turns and looks my way.

"He was in the driveway, by the way," she informs me. "I can't work out if you are the bad sister or the good one."

"The bad one. Oh boy, am I the bad one."

Noah walks up then and slides his hand around Rhianna's waist and leans down and kisses her cheek.

"What's going on?"

"August is here." He stops kissing her then swivels his head around until his eyes land on me. But we can only see my mother, as the wall blocks our view of the door.

"I should go over there," I say more to myself than anyone else.

"Yeah, you should save him before she chops his head off and feeds it to Anderson's parents," Rhianna says.

I turn to hand her the baby, but she has a drink in her hand, and the other is glued to Noah. I raise my brow at her, and she shrugs. "Aunty duties. You took him, so I'm having a twenty-minute break. Plus, the baby will help everything go smoothly," she adds.

"You really are evil. This is why Beckham is my favorite." I poke my tongue out at her.

"Please. He may be your favorite, but it's me who knows your soul."

Just as I turn to walk over with the baby, I see Winter run in and go straight for my father. He lifts and spins her around. Walking over to my mother, I hear the last bit of what she says to

August. "You can go now."

Giving August a quick perusal, his jeans don't meet the dress code for tonight. Everyone is dressed in suits and dresses, but I don't care.

"Come in. She's most likely just saying hi." I hand him her pink ballerina mouse, and he nods and takes one step closer to me. His eyes fall to the baby, and I offer him to August.

"Winter was the same size, but her length was a bit shorter."

"She was a small bundle of joy," my mother says, turning to see where Winter went.

I feel his eyes on me. "I should get going. We just needed to get the mouse, and, well..."

"It's no problem."

Anderson's mother walks over. Her eyes land on August, then swing to me. "What is he doing here?" she snaps.

Her husband, who is usually incredibly quiet, reaches for August and grabs him by the shirt, and starts pushing him out the back.

"What the hell?" Noah and Rhianna come straight up behind me, and I hand the baby to Rhianna and make my way to where Noah is pulling Anderson's father from August.

"You have some cheek showing your face here." My mother steps out of the doorway and shuts it behind her. Anderson's mother is standing on the doorstep with a sour expression written all over her face.

"What on earth are you doing? How dare you touch him?" I say, rushing over while holding my dress up so it doesn't drag along the ground.

Anderson's father looks to me and shakes his head. "You clearly need to keep better company. Was he fucking you the same time he was fucking my wife?" he practically screams in my face.

Confused, my eyes move from him to August. "What's he talking about?"

"I told you I did things to pay for food," he says, his hand kneading the back of his neck as he looks around. His eyes come back to me—regret and shame evident in their depths. "Things I'm not proud of," he says quietly.

"Mommy." We both turn to see Winter running in our direction. She goes to August and he picks her up. "We're going to play in the park, you should come." Her little voice is so innocent.

Green eyes lock on to mine. "Come over later. We can talk when she's asleep." August turns with her and heads to his car.

"That's probably not a good idea. Bring her back first thing in the morning," I tell him.

He starts to say something but thinks better of it.

I watch as they drive off and as I turn to leave Holden walks up. His smile is genuine, and it's obvious he has no idea what's going on. "Should we re-join the party?" he asks playfully.

I place my hand on his chest and smile up at him. "I don't think I'm quite ready for what you're looking for. I don't think we match the way I had hoped. I like you, so I want to tell you now before things become more serious between us."

The smile that was gracing his lips disappears. Holden steps back and looks around. Mostly everyone has gone back inside, apart from my mother, who is standing waiting for me, I presume.

"Could you take me home?" I ask Holden.

"Yes, of course."

"I'm sorry, Holden. I really am."

CHAPTER 21

August

Mary is sitting on the front porch when I get back, and Oliver is playing in the yard. When I stop the car, I turn to see Winter watching him.

"Would you like to go and play?" Winter nods eagerly at my words, and I get out to unbuckle her. As soon as she's out of the car, she runs straight over to him, and he hands her the bat he's hitting the ball with. I sit down next to Mary, and she doesn't make eye contact. She's hardly even spoken to me since the day Anderson was here.

"Winter is beautiful," she finally says, watching her playing with Oliver.

"She is," I agree.

I feel her eyes on me, and when I turn to face her, she offers me a soft smile. "She looks exactly like her."

I know what she's saying, and I agree, "She does."

"And you're still in love with her, even now, aren't you?"

"I am," I admit honestly.

I hear her take a deep breath next to me. "I guess I knew you wouldn't lie to me. It's one of the things that made me love you, August."

I reach my hand around her shoulder and pull her to me. "I love you too, Mary. I really do."

"I think ... well, I wonder, if perhaps I just love you as well, and I'm not *in love* with you. The problem is the pain says otherwise."

"Would you like to meet her?" I ask Mary, motioning to Winter, who is laughing at Oliver. She nods, and I call Winter over. She comes quickly and runs into my arms.

"Hi, my name is Mary. Can I ask yours?" Mary leans in close to me.

Winter lifts her head from my shoulder and stares at her. "Winter."

"Wow! Such a pretty name for a pretty girl," she says kindly. "I bet you love the winter too, right?"

Winter scrunches up her little nose at her. "I prefer summer, but that's my cousin's name, and she prefers winter, so..." She shrugs her shoulders like she can't work out why they have the wrong names.

Oliver calls Winter, she turns and runs back to him. He hands her the ball and they start to play again. I turn back to Mary to see her studying me.

"If I were a good woman, I would let you go. Be with her..." Her eyes lock onto mine as she stands with a deep sigh. "I'm already packed. Oliver and I have found somewhere to stay, but I wanted to meet Winter and to say goodbye to you."

I stand too and reach for Mary. My hands grip her hips, and I pull her to me and touch her face ever so softly. "You don't have to go," I tell her.

She smiles, but it never reaches her eyes. "I do, we both know it. I thank you so much for everything you did, August. You gave me a chance when I had no one." A tear leaves her eye. "You married me so I could change my name and they couldn't find me, and you showed Oliver what being a good person is." Mary leans up and kisses my cheek. "But I think it's time now that I do me and try to stop myself from falling completely in love with you. Because I am falling more and more in love with you each day."

"Mommy." We both turn to see Winter running up to her mother, who I didn't even hear pull up. It's dark outside, but she stands out under the night sky.

"It's the way you look at her that I want. I want someone to look at me the way you stare at her. You say she has soulless eyes, but I think you tell yourself that, so you don't fall deeper into them." Her lips peck me again before she pulls away and walks inside the house.

Winter pulls Rylee to where Oliver and I can hear her explaining what they're doing. Rylee's eyes find mine and hold, just for a brief second, before she reaches down and picks up our daughter and walks toward me. Oliver follows behind as Mary walks out holding a few bags in her arms.

"Are you going somewhere?" Rylee asks.

"I am. I found a cute little apartment not too far from here. Oliver and I are moving in there." Rylee looks back to Oliver and smiles.

"You don't have to go," I tell Mary again.

"I do. I really do."

I glance down to Mary's ring finger and see her wedding band is no longer there. It's not just me who notices that fact either. Rylee does too.

"Do you need any help?"

Mary pulls a bag up higher on her shoulder. "This would be a lot easier if you weren't so nice. I could make myself stay. But you are, and August..." Mary looks back to me. "Well, you know August."

Rylee stands there quietly, watching this all play out. I ask Rylee to take Winter inside while I help Mary pack her car. When the last bag is in, Oliver comes up to me and shakes my hand. He is growing up to be a great little man. I pull him in for a quick hug before he gets in the car.

"She still loves you, you know," Mary says, looking over my shoulder to the house.

I step up to her and cup her cheek. "Stay," I ask her.

Mary's head shakes in my hand, and she places her hand over mine. "It's not the right thing to do. We both know it. Take it slow with her. She may love you, but any woman can tell she is bruised from doing so." She pulls away and gets into her car, then drives off. I stand there until her taillights can no longer be seen before I turn around to go back inside.

Maybe I shouldn't have come back.

Maybe I should have stayed away.

Opening the front door, I see Winter and Rylee both curled up on the couch, asleep.

No, I definitely couldn't have stayed away.

Not from either of them.

CHAPTER 22

Rylee

I wake to a noise and tiptoe, so I don't wake Winter. Managing to get up in my long dress, I see August baking in the kitchen.

"She needs to go to bed," I tell him.

He turns to face me and brushes his hands on his shorts before he walks over, skimming right past me, and reaches for a sleeping Winter. I sit back down, my head in my hands, while I wait for him to come back out. When he does, he stands directly in front of me.

"You fucked Anderson's mother." I say the

words but don't want them to be true. They taste sour on my tongue.

"This ... this is why you were never meant to find out. Look at that judgment passing over your face right now."

He isn't wrong.

I am judging him.

It's hard not to.

"You fucked my ex's mother, and you forgot to tell me this?" I shake my head.

"I fucked a whole lot of people. Do you want a fucking list?" he snaps back.

I shake my head in disgust. He takes my chin between his thumb and forefinger, straightening it up. "See, in those dark eyes, you are judging so fucking hard."

I meet his angry gaze. "It's disgusting, on so many levels."

He doesn't let go of my chin. "You never seemed to complain when I fucked you."

I gasp at his words.

"Did my cock not meet your expectations?" he asks, as one side of his lip curls up. "Because if I remember clearly, you liked it when I fucked you. You liked it a lot."

"That's..." I pull back, so his fingers drop from my face, "... beside the point."

He smirks and steps closer to me. My heart rate picks up at his nearness, and I have to remember to breathe with him so close.

I may be disgusted with him, but I also love him.

That last part he doesn't need to know.

"It is the point. You say you're disgusted, but right now, dressed in that beautiful dress, I can see your nipples are erect just by being close to me."

I look down and see they are.

Shit.

"Do you want me to fuck you, perhaps? You know, considering I disgust you and all?"

"I..." Words fail me. August is right. I want him to touch me. There has never been a time since we met that I didn't want him to touch me. His touch softens me, heals me, makes me feel whole. August's touch is as wicked and beautiful as the night sky in a storm. You want to touch, feel, but you know it's dangerous. And like a storm chaser, you have to pursue until you're lost in his vortex.

"Last chance to run." August captures me before I can utter another word, his hands pulling me to him, and my body smashes into him.

I should be saying no.

I should be stopping this.

But it would be like trying to stop a speeding train with my bare hands. Impossible.

His mouth touches me first, and when his lips meet mine, I freeze in that moment to take it all in.

That's what it's like to be kissed by someone you love.

Magical.

It's soft, tender, but also hard and full of need.

His hands grip my hips, and he pulls me to him, holding me in place so if I wanted to move, only he could give me the permission to do so.

And I am not going to complain. Not in the slightest.

I've missed those hands.

Five long years of not having those hands on me.

I kiss him back. I'm helpless not to. Just as I go to reach for his face to keep his lips on mine, he pulls back, hands and lips leaving me as he steps around me. I stay frozen in place. His hands caress the back of my dress, and he ever so slowly removes it and lets it drop to the floor. I feel his eyes on me, eating me alive.

Is he judging me?

My body is different now.

It's full of wear and tear and tells a story of where I housed a beautiful child.

When I glance up at him, I can tell he doesn't see me any differently. He simply wants me.

I shake my head. No, this isn't right.

He fucked Anderson's mother. *What the actual fuck?*

Before I can move or even reach for my dress, his shirt is off and he's in front of me, his hands cupping my bare ass as he lifts me, so my legs have to wrap around his waist.

I shouldn't want him after what I learned tonight.

So why do I?

Maybe, for now, I can forget.

Maybe, for now, I won't think of how his wife just walked out.

Maybe, for now, I won't think how bad, so very bad, this is.

I've loved him for a long time, and I think, no matter what, I always will. Even when he breaks my heart.

My back hits the wall, and he reaches between us, one hand still holding me up. I feel him maneuver his jeans out of the way and then I feel him. Right there.

I probably should have worn panties. Maybe

that would have given me time—time for me to stop this.

Would I, though? I'm not really sure.

His finger finds my clit and he rubs it as his mouth fits to mine perfectly. I gasp with pleasure as his finger picks up speed, and before I can say anything else, I feel him enter me. Fast. Hard. And demanding.

He gives me a moment to catch my breath before both hands are under my ass, holding me up and his mouth falls to my breast. He licks my nipple before he takes it between his teeth and tugs it. I moan, and he repeats the motion on the other one. My body can't stand being still, so I lift ever so slightly to get some movement and friction, my body knowing full well what it wants.

This is nothing like being with Holden. No, I'm not sure Holden knows how to please a woman. Despite all his best features, that one thing is a massive flaw.

August knows my body. How? I don't really want to know. I'm not sure I'll like the answer.

"Rich girl." He says my name, and my eyes snap to his. He smirks as he starts moving me up and down, his rhythm never slowing. "I've missed you, rich girl." I look away, and he leans in and bites my neck before he soothes it with kisses.

I can't look into those eyes and tell him I've missed him too.

He can see I still love him. That I haven't just missed him, I have craved him. And that's not fair. It's not fair at all.

I hug him to me, my head falling to the crook of his neck as I bite him back. I kiss him there, and he doesn't stop the pleasure. The friction of his body against my clit is making it hard to hold back. I dig my nails into his shoulders to try to ground myself. He laughs, knowing full well what's happening before I stop trying and let it wash over me.

And there it is.

An orgasm.

One I didn't have to give myself.

It's been a long time.

August holds me to him, and I get the feeling he doesn't want to let me go. And I'm not sure what will happen when he does.

This shouldn't have happened.

I shouldn't have fucked a married man.

Oh, my God, he and his wife just broke up.

Fuck.

Fuck.

Fuck.

What does that make me?

Am I the other woman?

Am I a whore?

I would never hurt someone, not on purpose or indirectly if I can help it. This isn't me. I shouldn't have come over. I should have stayed at my apartment and waited for August to bring Winter back tomorrow morning. But, like a fool, I came here hoping for something, and now I have more than I ever thought about.

I go to pull away, but he holds me to him.

"August, let me go," I plead in a whisper.

"No can do, rich girl," he says, then kisses my neck.

"August," I say again. "I need to go."

"Do you really, or are you just freaking out right now? It will pass. I'll hold you through it."

I take in his words and then shake my head and pull back. My legs drop to the floor, and we stand in front of each other, naked. He goes to reach for me again, but I step back.

"We never should have done this," I state, rubbing my hands down my face. "Oh, my God, you're married," I say with a heavy breath. "What we did was so wrong."

"Mary and I haven't had sex for months."

I look into his green eyes and shake my head.

"That doesn't make it any better. I saw the way she looked at you. I look at you the same way, August. She loves you."

"You love me, rich girl?" He smirks, still very much naked and very handsome.

"Arghhh," I scream. His body is better than it was five years ago. How is that even possible? It's more defined, his arms are more significant, the veins in them even more lickable. "You love her too, right?" I ask him.

"I love her, yes."

My heart cracks at his words.

I literally feel it.

Like someone split it open.

"But not in the way I love you."

"I have to go. I have to." I look around for my dress, find it on the floor, and pull it over my head. It falls down my body like a waterfall, and I look up the stairs to where Winter is sleeping.

"She's asleep." Somehow, he moved to me without me knowing and is now standing in front of me. I glance down to where his jeans are lying on the floor.

"I have to go."

"Rich girl." He reaches for my face, but I step back so he can't touch me again. That is not allowed. Because I am defenseless to his touch, and it's entirely unfair.

"Kiss Winter for me. I'll see you tomorrow," I say, trying to make my escape. His hand captures my arm before I can leave. And when I peer back at him, his eyes lock with mine.

"It's always been you. Never anyone else. Always you, rich girl."

"Then why did you leave?" I bite back. "Clearly, it wasn't right. We aren't right. For fuck's sake, August, you should have told me you fucked his mother. You really do bring a whole new meaning to motherfucker." I pull my arm free and open his front door.

Storming out, I get to my car and slide in. I don't look back. It's a stupid thing to do, just as it was foolish to open my legs for him.

I bang my hands on the wheel and swear at myself.

How could I be so stupid?

Why?

CHAPTER
2 3

August

Sleeping was next to impossible. Instead, I went out back to the same place where I used to build everything, to the place where I find my peace. I've only been in here once since I've been home, and that was to make Winter's bedroom furniture. My hand runs along the wood, itching for me to make something, anything.

"Auggie." I snap my head up to see Winter standing at the door. She's rubbing her eyes, so I go to her and pick her up and kiss her cheek. "I'm hungry."

"Well, we have to feed the monster or the monster might come out and eat us," I say, grabbing her belly and making her laugh. Back in the kitchen, I place her at the counter and start her pancakes.

"Uncle Benji says you're a dickhead. What's a dickhead?" she says, making me pause mid-stir of the batter. I turn to see her watching me, a crayon in her hand is paused over a coloring book.

"Ignore that. He shouldn't be using those words around you."

"Oh, he didn't. He said it to Mommy." She smiles and goes back to coloring.

Reaching for my phone because it dings, Rylee's message asks what time she should pick up Winter. I call her because even after all this time, I still hate texting. And let's face it, I would rather listen to her voice anytime. "You're on speaker," I tell her as I place the phone down.

"Hey, so what time should I come today?"

I pause and look back to Winter. "Why don't you come now and have breakfast with us?" I ask her.

Winter looks up and smiles. "Yeah, Mommy, come."

"Way to put me on the spot." I smirk at her words. "Okay, I'll be there in ten."

"Goodbye, rich girl."

"Don't you start," she snaps, then hangs up the phone.

"How many pancakes today?" I ask Winter, a grin breaking over my face. Winter holds up both hands, and I get to cooking her ten pancakes, as requested.

Rylee arrives in five minutes, not ten. She's dressed in a summer dress that stops above her knees, and her dark hair is tied up. She pulls her sunglasses from her head when she walks inside and flicks her eyes to me before she sits down next to Winter.

"Did you save me any?" she asks Winter, smiling. She nods and points to the stack I just finished. "Oh, so sweet." Rylee looks up at me as I bite my lip, and her eyes go straight to it. She tries and fails to fight her smile.

"Do you want cream and strawberries?" I ask then smirk.

"No, pancakes and syrup will do."

"Are you sure?" I step closer, carrying the plate of pancakes. "Winter, why don't you go and get dressed, then bring your bag down?" I say to her, all the while staring at what I want for breakfast.

We watch as Winter jumps up and runs up the stairs.

"I could lift that dress and have my breakfast," I say as I squeeze some of the cream onto my plate.

"Oh gosh, fuck off." She shakes her head.

"Listen to you. I bet you only have a potty mouth for me."

"You are correct," she snaps back.

"Do you ever wonder why that is?"

"August." We both turn at the sound of his name being called from the front door.

I hardly recognize the woman who stands on the other side. She looks different. Her eyes flit over me for a few seconds, then fall to Rylee, who stands next to me.

"You two are back together?" my mother asks, looking between us.

"No," Rylee answers first. I watch my mother as she tucks a strand of hair behind her ear and smiles at me.

"I wanted to give you time, but I had heard you were back. Is it okay that I'm here?" She never would have asked that before. She's dressed in an apron, and her hair is tied up. She runs her hands over her outfit after noticing my gaze. "Sorry, I came straight from work at the café."

"You're working? That's great," Rylee says, smiling.

How can she do that, switch so easily?

"You should get going," I say to Rylee. Her mouth forms an O, and before she can do or say anything, Winter comes down with her bag in her hand to the front door. I watch as my mother's eyes fall to her when she walks up and hugs Rylee's leg.

"Oh, who is this?" My mother drops down in a crouch to get on the same level as Winter.

Rylee turns to me, unsure of what to say.

"This is Winter," I reply.

She holds out her hand to Winter and smiles warmly. "It's nice to meet you, Winter."

"It's Winter Paige," Winter tells her, and my mother gasps before she stands back up.

Rylee lifts Winter and looks at me. "We're going to go. I have a few things I need to get done."

"She yours?" my mother asks Rylee.

"She is," she replies proudly.

"She has your eyes, August," my mother states, looking back at me. I nod in response. It's all I can do. Rylee excuses herself as she goes to grab her things, leaving me standing there with my mother.

"I didn't think you wanted kids," she says softly.

"Neither did I. I guess things change."

"Yes, indeed, they do." We both turn as Rylee and Winter return to me.

"It was great seeing you. You're looking good," Rylee says to Mom, then smiles at me and walks out of the house. I follow her to the car and take Winter, placing her inside the car then kissing her cheek. I tell her I'll see her next weekend and close the door.

"Be nice," Rylee says, looking back to where my mother is standing near the doorway.

"Oh, so you hate me but want to tell me to be nice to her?" I bark back at Rylee. I want to inch closer and see if I can retake a taste of her lips. It's all I crave right now.

"I don't hate you. I never could. I'm just..." She shivers and shakes her head. "Never mind, I have to go."

Rylee gets in the car and rolls her window down. I lean over and whisper so only she can hear, "I'll be dreaming of all the ways you scream my name." Her eyes go wide, and I pull away, walking back to the house.

My mother stays where she is and waits for me to walk back to her, then we watch as Rylee pulls out of the driveway. As she goes, my mother turns to me and states categorically, "You love that girl." I don't need to ask her which one she's talking about to know. "You both created a gorgeous daughter."

"I think so," I say while opening the front door. "Would you like to come in for a coffee?" Her eyes flick to my hand and she zeros in on my ring.

"Your wife won't mind?"

I look down and realize I haven't taken it off. "She left."

My mother nods and doesn't ask any more questions.

"I knew you would always find your way back here for her. I just had to wait," she utters as she walks in.

Find my way back to her.

My biggest mistake.

Because I should never have left.

CHAPTER 24

Rylee

August calls during the week. Our conversations are short. He asks me about Winter, and we leave it at that. I don't bring up what happened between us, and thankfully, he doesn't either.

I'm still a little disgusted by it all, if I am honest.

How could he do that? Sleep with Anderson's mother. *What the fuck?*

When I walk out of work, Anderson's mother is standing there. Her phone is to her ear as she looks up at me. I duck my head and try to walk past her, but she steps in front of me and blocks my path, making me raise my eyes to hers. Shandy walks up behind me and touches my shoulder.

Anderson's mother eyes her. "Give us a minute, girl."

Shandy is about to laugh at her words until I turn around and nod to her. Shandy concedes and says, "I'll be by your car. Call if you need me."

"She won't."

"What can I help you with, Mrs. Lee?"

"You chose that boy, that disgusting boy, over *my son*." She wrinkles her nose up at me.

"He mustn't have been too disgusting for you to fuck him," I bite back. Her face goes red with embarrassment, and I am proud that I can speak so openly like this. Something I have never been able to do before. This woman must think I have no backbone. Well, she is dead wrong. It was purely out of respect when I was with Anderson. And now? Well, she doesn't have any sort of respect from me—the opposite, actually.

"How dare you, child? Who do you think you are?"

"I'm whoever the fuck I want to be. How about next time, you don't cheat on your husband and keep your hands to yourself." I turn to leave, but her voice stops me.

"How much did he charge you? Because I would have paid more. I mean, he is good, isn't he?"

I turn around and stalk straight over, pulling up right in her face. "You are sick. Fucking sick. You know that, right? August doesn't charge me. He loves me. There is a difference. You..." I spit, eyeing her up and down, "... were simply a way to feed himself. Don't think for a second he would have chosen you when he could have this." I turn and walk away from her, my fists bunched up, wanting to punch her in the face but refraining because that is not me.

"Rylee."

I roll my eyes when I see Anderson standing in front of me.

Can this day get any worse?

Anderson looks past me to his mother, then back to me.

"I can't blame you for being such a fuckwit anymore, Anderson. It comes from your mother," I yell.

Anderson scrunches up his nose in confusion. "Rylee." He goes to reach for me, but I pull back. I never, ever want to feel his touch on me again. "I have a son. Did you know that?" He changes the subject. Then his face goes hard as his eyes narrow in on me. "And your boyfriend is keeping him from me."

"That's wrong, and you know it." I go to walk away, but he steps in front of me, blocking my path.

"Tell August I'll be seeing him. I'm not the same man I was five years ago. He no longer scares me." Anderson smirks and steps around me, going to his mother's side, then looks back. "I never thought I could be disgusted with you until I heard you fucked the same man that fucked my mother. That is wrong. So, so wrong."

His mother turns up her nose as if she is pleased with this ignoramus' words.

Seriously, that family is all kinds of fucked up and then some more.

"Hey, I saw your ex. Are you okay?" Shandy walks up behind me and looks to where they are walking away.

"How was I ever with someone so totally wrong for me?" I ask as I turn to her.

"We all make mistakes. You know better now, and that's all that matters."

I've thought about this situation a lot.

Dealing with August.

And none of it went as I had imagined. It all went worse. Way worse.

"Do you plan to sit there and ignore me?" my mother asks as we sit at the table for a family dinner. She still insists we have them, so we all agreed to one night a month. Beckham smirks at me, knowing I want to ignore her, but now she's called me out on it, I won't. I turn and see the girls sitting at the smaller table my mother got for them. They're playing with Barbies as they eat.

"The possibility is there."

"Stop smiling at your sister." A napkin is thrown at Beckham's head, and he rubs the spot as if it hurt him, but of course, it didn't. "I didn't invite them here. They showed up."

"I'm sure that's how it went."

"I also didn't tell August to sleep with her." Rhianna chokes on her drink on the other side of me as my eyes go wide. "Really, Rylee, there is no need to be angry at me. I think this is a good thing. Now you know what type of person he really is." I push my seat back and reach for my phone, then walk out the door as my mother calls my name.

"She didn't take Winter. Just relax, she'll be back," I hear Rhianna say to my mother.

Stepping outside, I press call, and August picks up on the second ring. "I need you to do me a favor. You owe me."

"What do you need?"

"Come to my parents' house. We're having dinner. I'll save you a plate."

"Rich girl." He tries to argue with his term of endearment thrown my way, but I will not take no for an answer this time. "Nope. Come now. You put us in this mess, you can get us the hell out of it. If not for me, then do it at least for our daughter."

I hear him huff into the phone, then the jangle of his keys. "I would've done it for you." He hangs up, and I know he's on his way.

I walk back inside and slide my phone into my pocket.

"Good, you're back," my mother says. "Now, what do you plan to do about the situation?"

"You should set another seat. Noah is coming over."

Rhianna looks at me, knowing he's sleeping with the baby. She turned on the nanny cam before and saw him snuggled up in the rocking chair with their little boy lying on him as he slept. She wanted to call to wake them, but the baby hasn't been sleeping well and neither has Noah.

I watch as Mother gets up and prepares another plate. I drink my wine as Rhianna raises her brows at me, and I simply offer her a small smirk as I wait.

It doesn't take August long, and when I hear

the chime of the doorbell, I get up to answer it before anyone else can. I open the door and there stands August, dressed in black slacks and a button-up shirt looking fine.

"You didn't have to dress up for this," I tell him, holding the door open wider.

"I was in the process of meeting clients," he says, pulling at his tie.

"For your woodwork?" I ask, hopeful.

"Yes. Now, am I going to regret this?"

I nod, smiling. "Yes." I smirk. "Yes, you are."

"That smile is positively evil," he says, as I shut the door and nod for him to follow me through the house. As soon as we walk into the dining room, Winter spots August and runs over to him, her little arms wrapping around his legs in a tight hold.

"Auggie, you're here," Winter says, pulling back and holding out her hands for him to pick her up. He does and kisses her cheek, beaming at her like she is the best thing that has ever happened to him. I like that smile. It makes my stomach flutter, and want to fly away.

Mother's face is red, her lips are in a long thin line, and she looks like she's ready to explode.

"Look, Mother, now August is here to tell you *all about* his wicked ways." August glares at me as I place a hand on his shoulder and pat it.

"Good luck to you." I clap for Winter and she comes to me then I walk her back to her table, out of earshot, and tell her to eat before I step back to the dining room. August is standing at the table, looking unsure, putting his weight on one leg then the other. I take my seat and pull out the chair between myself and Rhianna and tell him to sit. He eyes it, and I can tell he wants to fight me but sits anyway.

"I thought, instead of asking me about August, you can ask him directly. That way you can stop..." I pin my mother with a glare, "... asking me. How does that sound?" I smile and reach for my wine.

"You should have asked first," Mother says through firmly gritted teeth.

"There is no fun in that, and he's here now. And August wants to answer all your questions." I look at him. "Don't you, August? My mother is genuinely concerned about what you did. You know ... with Mrs. Lee all those years ago."

August coughs uncomfortably, and those beautiful green eyes lock on to mine, with promises of payback shining in their depths.

"Yes, August, why don't you tell us what you did to Anderson's mother?" Beckham chimes in.

Rhianna hits him in the arm. "You shut up. You are the biggest slut of them all. You have no right to talk." Rhianna looks to August. "You don't have to answer them."

"Rhianna," our mother scolds, narrowing her eyes at her.

I hand him the salad, and he puts some on his plate before I hand him the meat. "Eat. You'll need your energy," I tell him, smirking.

He raises one brow at me, but it's not for what he thinks. I glance down the table to my mother who is watching us with drawn eyebrows.

"Why don't you ask him?" I say to my mother.

The table goes quiet as I standoff with her.

"You wanted to know why he fucked Mrs. Lee ... so, ask him. He's going to be in my life because he is Winter's father, and no one can change that."

"You don't have to tell us anything, son," my father says, holding up his drink and nodding to him. I appreciate that Dad is willing to let August's past lie, but I'm not just doing this for my mother. I need to hear it too.

"No, he does. I want to know why," Mother insists.

"Mom," Rhianna says.

"What? I need to know that the man who is going to be around my daughter is good and that the father of my granddaughter is going to teach her right from wrong and not allow her to sleep with strangers," she spits.

"Mrs. Lee made me an offer I couldn't refuse, and she knew it." We all turn our attention to August as he speaks, but he addresses my mother when he does.

"I highly doubt that." My mother straightens herself in her chair, waiting for him to continue. "No one can be that desperate, surely?"

"That just shows you have lived a life of privilege, and you would never understand what it's like to try to feed yourself because your mother can't be bothered to take care of you any longer."

"Again, you don't have to explain yourself, son," my father says. "As long as you are there for my child and grandchild, I don't care what you did in your past. The past is just that, the past." He nods to him.

"But that's not enough for you, is it, Mrs. Harley?"

My mother shakes her head. She has no shame at all in admitting it.

"I found a way to feed myself at a young age. When my mother stopped buying food, it was either that or starve to death. You don't really get a choice when you're that hungry that the gnawing hunger pangs are eating at your very soul. I had to find a way to make money to buy shoes, to get to school, to live even if it was wrong..." He pauses. "I was working for a guy named Josh. I had just started when Mrs. Lee first saw me. She asked why my shoes were so broken. I shrugged and told her I didn't have the money to buy a new pair." He takes a deep breath, then continues, "She bought me a pair, then asked me to come back to her house to shower."

"August," I say, looking at him.

"I thought nothing of it. Our shower hadn't been working for close to a week ... the water was disconnected. I was washing using the taps at school, but that didn't do the job. Plus, she was Anderson's mother, and I thought maybe she wasn't such a bitch like her son. I thought wrong—"

"She most certainly is," Beckham breaks in.

"I showered, and when I got out, my clothes were gone, and she was standing there, dressed in a nightgown." He swallows. "She offered me new clothes as well as more shoes. Nikes. I was a teenager, and all my friends had Nikes, apart from me. Then she offered me money. She said in order for me to get all those things, there was one thing she wanted from me."

Everybody stays quiet as we wait for him to speak again.

"She wanted me. And if I continued to sleep with her, she would shower me with all my wildest dreams." August lowers his eyes to his food, then raises them back up to my mother. "You don't know what kind of offer that is to someone who's never had anything. Plus, I liked sex. I was a teenager. It wasn't so bad."

"That's rape, son," my father growls, his face now a mask of anger.

"I knew that. So I told myself after that first time that I'd never do it again, but then..." he looks to me, "... she gave me a bike and offered more money as long as I did it again."

"Now you understand why Anderson is such a pig," Beckham says to our mother, who is just sitting there taking it all in. Mom's quiet now. No more smug looks, no more judgment in her eyes, only somber stillness.

I was angry at August before, knowing what he has done. But as I turn to look at him now, it's hard to stay mad at someone for something they never had any sort of control over. He was young, hungry, and desperate, so who can blame him for someone misleading him in such a horrific manner.

"I'm sorry," I tell him, tears welling in my eyes for the boy he had been. The boy who was forced to become a man simply because his mother was too fucked up to care. August's hand slides under the table to squeeze my leg.

"That woman is never allowed in this house again." My mother stands, pushing her chair back, and walks to the kitchen.

My father's eyes follow her, then he looks at August. "Please know, she is hard because she cares."

And that's a nice way to say she's a bitch, but once she loves you, she will fight tooth and nail for you. Even if she doesn't know whether it's wrong or right.

She isn't all that bad, but sometimes she just doesn't see the world as clearly as she should.

CHAPTER 25

August

"I'll be a minute." I stand and follow Rylee's mother to the kitchen. I see her standing by the sink, her hands on either side, holding on, looking out the window to the night sky in contemplation.

"I wanted to hate you," she says, somehow knowing it's me. She turns to face me, and a tear leaves her eye, and she wipes it away so fast you wouldn't even know it was there. "Rylee hasn't moved on since you left. I thought with Holden, it could have happened." I see so much of her daughter in her when I look at her. "But just as I love her father, I'm sure she loves you. I want you to know I wouldn't have chosen you, August. Not at all. She deserves the world, and I wanted that for her. And you aren't the world. You can't buy her all the things she might want. But maybe, you are *her* world."

"I didn't come back to win her back," I tell her, and her eyes go wide in surprise. "I didn't come back to stay until I saw Winter. It was then I knew I had to. I may have been given a mother who never cared for me, but I knew when I saw Winter, I could never be an absent father. I already had been ... although unknowingly, and it killed me to know I had missed so much already. I love them both. And even if Rylee will never want me back, I will still be here, no matter what."

"I hope you're right because I will hunt you down and kill you if you break either of those girls' hearts."

I smile at her words. "Now, what do you want me to do?" I look around, offering my help.

"Do for what?" she asks, confused.

"Clean. Cook."

Mrs. Harley laughs. "Nothing. But it is getting late, so you may want to take the girls home."

When I walk back out, the table is being cleared as Rylee kisses her sister and Summer goodbye. Rhianna offers me a wave as she steps out, and Beckham comes to stand next to me. "I don't like you," he states matter-of-factly, making me turn to him.

"I don't need you to like me."

Beckham huffs at my response. "You are a dick," Beckham says. "But even though you seem to have changed, I have a feeling you would still put me in my grave." He winks. "Doesn't mean I wouldn't take you with me, though." He walks over to Winter, and she jumps into his ready arms. I guess that's something I have to get used to, sharing my daughter with family. I've never had a family, apart from Paige, and even then, I only saw her briefly.

"Let me follow you home," I say to Rylee.

"Are you sure?" she asks.

Their father walks up and holds out his hand, and as I shake it, he pulls me in for a one-arm hug. "Welcome to the family, son." He pulls away and hugs Winter and gives her money. I look back to Rylee to see her smiling.

"Word of warning. Papa, as Winter likes to call him, loves to shower her with money. I've tried to stop it, but it's useless. So, she takes it and adds to her piggy bank." Rylee nudges me with her arm. "They like you. I knew they would once they got to know you."

Winter is asleep by the time we arrive at Rylee's place. I wait out front on the apartment steps as she takes her inside to bed. When she comes back out, she's holding two glasses of wine and sits next to me, handing me one.

"I kind of threw you in the deep end, hey?" Rylee says with a mischievous grin. Her lips are pink tonight. Natural. Her eyes dark and spectacular. How did I ever think they were soulless? They aren't. They hold so much life, so much hope—more than I could ever contain.

"You did, but I'm glad you did it."

"Me, too. Now you can come to all the parties, especially when they involve Winter. You should have seen the first birthday party Mother threw for Winter." She shakes her head.

"I missed a lot," I reply, gazing back out to the night sky.

"You did, but you're here now. She will remember that. So don't fuck it up," she warns me.

We sit in comfortable silence together for a few moments, then she speaks, breaking it. "What did you do while you were gone? You used to at least answer my calls at the beginning, then stopped."

"I got a job at a factory, stayed in a motel. For

the first six months, I did just that. Nothing else. My hands never touched wood again, not until I came back here."

"How about Jacinta? How did you meet her?"

I smile at the memory. "She applied for a job at the factory. I was the one who interviewed her. And then, I asked her where she was living. At the time, she was in a home trying to keep her name off everything. So, I gave her a job, found a place for me to live, then asked her if she wanted to move in with me." I turn to see her watching me. "It never started off as anything other than friendship. It took years to even get anywhere. She wanted to enroll Oliver in school, but not under her name, so I offered to marry her, and she changed her name."

"Do you miss her?"

"I miss talking to her. She's a good woman. You two would actually get along. But she knew I never loved her the way she wanted me to. I tried. I really did. But..."

"I tried, too. I tried so many times to move on," she shares with me. "They say you have three great loves in your lifetime, but what if all my great loves are the same person?"

"I could never be anyone's great love," I tell her.

"Am I not yours?"

I reach up and caress her face, and she leans

into my touch. "I know I only have one, and you are it. I've known it for a long time."

"So why did you leave?" she asks.

"I wasn't in my right mind. And staying meant I would have eventually ended up back where I didn't want to go. I did some dark shit, and I would do it again for the same outcome, rich girl, even if it meant I had to lose you in the process. They took someone from me I will never get back."

Her head leans on my shoulder. "You could have come back."

"I was angry for so long. So damn angry. I couldn't have. And by the time I wasn't as angry, I had met Mary, and she needed me. You have never needed me, rich girl. You never needed anyone. You had to know that as well."

"I would have liked the opportunity to need you."

Leaving my wine glass on the ground while hers is still clutched in her hand, I stand and pull her up with me. "Rich girl." I push a strand of hair out of her face, and just as I do, a loud bang rings through the quiet night air. Rylee's eyes go wide, her face turns white, then the glass in her hand falls to the ground and shatters at our feet. I feel her start to drop and catch her before she can fall. "Rylee."

I hear manic laughter behind her, and what I

see tells me I am just about to go back on everything I've ever said.

I'm going straight back to prison.

But before I do, Anderson *will* be going in the ground.

"You took what was mine, so now I am taking what's yours." Anderson saunters off like he doesn't have a care in the world, and I look down at Rylee, whose eyes are wide in fear as she struggles to breathe.

Fuck. I lay her down ever so gently on the ground and pull out my phone, and dial for an ambulance. They tell me they're on the way as I watch the blood pool around her.

"Rich girl, stay with me." I hear the sirens and look back to her apartment. Fuck! Winter. Reaching for my phone again with blood-covered hands, I call Beckham, and he answers straight away. "Get to your sister's, now," I yell at him through the phone.

"Who the fuck do you think—"

"Rylee's been shot. Hurry."

Beckham hangs up, and I know he will be here soon.

The ambulance arrives and Rylee's eyes are closed, her breathing shallow, as they check her over and start moving. I watch helplessly as they stabilize her, then put her into the back and drive away. I stand there, blood-soaked hands itching to scrub my face.

I can't lose another person I love.

I won't.

Not again.

"August." I raise my head to see Beckham standing in front of me. "No, don't you dare. Don't even think about it. Do you want to go away for life and never see Winter again?" he bellows. I realize my hands are in fists and my mouth tight as I breathe heavily. "Winter inside?" he asks, motioning to the house.

I manage a nod, and he places a hand on my shoulder. "Go to the hospital. I got Winter. Mom and Dad will meet you there."

Hospital. Yeah, right.

How about no?

Pulling my keys from my pocket, I feel my heart break in my chest.

I knew where he would be. It was more than evident to me. Anderson is an asshole who will never change, no matter how many times you beat him senseless. The gun he used is nowhere in sight as I walk up to him. He holds a beer in his hand as he laughs at something someone said. *How dare he sit there like he didn't just shoot the love of my life?*

It takes one knock to the back of his head to send him crashing to the ground, the beer going with him, cutting his hands up as he falls. He screams like the little bitch he is as he turns to face me. I kick him hard in the stomach, making him scream even louder and fall onto his back.

"If she dies, you know you *will* soon follow," I tell him, leaning down and grabbing his shirt so I am in his face. He goes to punch me but misses, and I strike him in the face, hearing and feeling the crack of his nose underneath my fist.

Hands wrap around me, pulling me back, but I push and lurch forward, my hands extending toward Anderson again and hitting him once more.

"August." Strong arms wrap around me, and this time, I'm unable to move. "You need to calm down and tell me whose blood that is." Anderson is restrained on the ground by a police officer who's looking up at me.

"He has a gun on him," I tell him.

The police officer pats down Anderson's body until he finds the gun and pulls it free.

"How did you know that?" I turn to see Glenn behind me. I haven't seen him in so long. He looks older, more worn down since I last laid eyes on me. "August, whose blood is that?"

"Rylee's," I answer.

"Where is she?" he asks.

"Hospital."

He nods. "Go. And don't come back. You were never here." I look around to see all the police officers surrounding Anderson, their guns trained on him. "I've seen her, by the way. She's beautiful ... Winter," he finishes, offering me a small smile.

With my hands still clenched in fists and bloodied, all I can do is nod and walk out.

CHAPTER
26

Rylee

I wake to voices. Lots of voices. A hand tightly clutching mine. When I manage to open my eyes, I see my sister by my side, her eyes puffy and red with tears as she sits there staring off at nothing.

"Rhi." My voice is dry and scratchy, and I lick my lips as she jumps from her seat to hover over me.

"Oh, my God..." She lets go of my hand and runs from the room.

When she comes back, a doctor is with her,

and he smiles down at me. "It's good to finally meet you, Rylee." I try to smile, but my eyes want to shut. "You did great and are expected to make a full recovery. The bullet missed any major organs, but we had to operate to get it out. You'll be sore for some time, and I will discuss it more later when I come back to see you."

"Mommy." My eyes spring open at that voice. Winter is next to me and looking down at me as August holds her. She reaches for me, but August pulls her back. "Mommy needs to rest right now, but tomorrow, we'll come back and see how she is."

"August."

His eyes are tired, and I think mine more than likely match his.

"She will be fine. She's been fine," August says.

August shuffles out, and as he does, I notice my brother sitting in one of the seats near the window. "He beat him, put him in the hospital," Beckham says as I watch him groggily. "I should have done it, but August got to him first. Anderson," he adds, telling me who he's talking about—as if I didn't know.

"He can't," I say, shaking my head.

August can't go back to where he was.

Especially now.

He has a family.

"Glenn was there, and he covered for him."

I sigh. *That's a relief.*

"Where is Anderson now?"

"At the police station. I don't think he can get away from this one so easily. They found the gun, and now they have the forensic evidence with the bullet from you. Mommy and Daddy's money won't be able to save him from this."

"That's good to hear. I'm just going to rest my eyes."

Blackness overtakes me quickly as I flutter my eyes and go back to sleep.

I wake again to a soft voice. As my eyes adjust, I see Jacinta standing there with her son. It's late and no one else is here.

"Jacinta." She jumps when I say her name but smiles down at me.

"I'm sorry. I'm sorry that you keep getting the shit end of the stick. I'm sorry for running." She shakes her head. "Maybe if I stayed, he wouldn't have been so mad at you. At August."

"No, it was bound to happen. None of this is your fault."

She smiles and holds her son's hand. He looks

like Anderson, but he has more of his mother's features.

"Anderson's father called. Said I should never bring Oliver around his wife, and that he will pay for a lawyer to draw me up papers saying that I have full custody."

My eyes go wide at her words.

"He's also leaving Mrs. Lee, and he asked if he could see Oliver from time to time if I will allow it."

Anderson's dad was probably the only normal one in the family. I say nothing at her revelation. She doesn't need me to. It's her decision to decide who sees her son and who doesn't.

"August has loved you for so long. I want you to know that. I wanted him to love me. I would have been happy with just a fraction of the love he has for you." A tear escapes her eye, and she wipes it away.

"Jacinta."

"It's okay, I get it. He isn't *my* love, but that doesn't mean you two can't make it work. August started building things again. He never did that when he was with me. It's because you make him happy, and you give him hope when he thought he had none."

I go to say something, but Oliver pulls on her hand and she leans down to listen to him. When she stands back up, she smiles.

"I got a job at your office. I wanted you to be the first to know so when you see me, you won't think I'm stalking you," she says. "I'll be assisting someone by the name of Beckham."

"I'm happy for you. I'm sure you'll do great." My eyes become heavy again, and I yawn.

They both say goodbye and wish me a speedy recovery before they leave.

When I wake up again, my head doesn't feel so heavy, and my stomach grumbles.

"Are you hungry?" I turn to see August in the seat next to my bed. He sits up and rubs his eyes as he looks at me.

"Yes."

He gets up, stretches his legs, and I can't help but stare as he does. I watch as he walks to the door and then comes back and touches the side of the bed, making it lift, so I'm in more of a sitting position.

I go to move and feel a twinge of pain in my back. "Fuck."

"Don't move. Let me know if you need to and I'll help."

"You a doctor now?"

August takes over helping me sit and puts a

pillow behind my back.

"Where is Winter?"

"I dropped her off a few hours ago with Beckham. Your sister offered, but she looks so tired."

"Beckham is who she will prefer to be with anyway."

He nods and retakes his seat. "I figured as much," he replies, as a woman brings in a tray of food, sets it on the overbed table, then walks out. He pulls off the cloche and gets it ready for me as if I'm a toddler. I smile as I watch him fiddle around then he hands me the fork.

His eyes lock on to mine. "What?"

"You are a good man, you know that, right?"

"It's only you who believes that, rich girl."

"No, it's not only me. And I'm sure many have told you." He ignores me and sits back. "Why are you here so late?" I ask him, lifting the jelly and taking a mouthful. It tastes bland, but the last thing I want to do is upset my stomach, so I eat it happily. "And how long have I been asleep?"

"It's been two days since you were admitted, and you have been asleep on and off since that time. I spent the day with Winter, and now I'm spending the night with you."

We both go silent and sit there and eat. When I'm done, he moves the tray away and goes to adjust my bed to lay me back down, but I shake my head.

"You need to rest."

"I'll be fine. I'm awake now." He sits back down and lifts one leg so it sits across his knee as he leans back and watches me. "Jacinta was here," I tell him, not sure if they are talking. I peek at his hand. He is no longer wearing his wedding ring.

"That was nice of her."

"You don't care to ask why?" I ask.

"No. I know she would never have bad intentions."

I take a deep breath. It hurts. I wince, and he's up next to me straight away.

"I'm fine." I brush him off. "Sit." He does but doesn't stop watching and assessing me. "She got a job with Beckham. I don't think she knows he's my brother yet, and I am sure she has no idea what an ass he is to work for."

He just nods at my words.

"Are you just going to continue to stare at me?"

"Yes," he answers truthfully.

"How did it go with your mom?" I ask, changing the subject. He moves just slightly, but it's enough for me to notice. I guess the question makes him uncomfortable.

"Fine."

I roll my eyes at his words. "Tell me more. How did it go? She seemed better."

"You should rest," he informs me.

"And you should tell me."

"She is better. She's been clean for almost five years."

A soft yawn leaves my mouth. "You can put my bed down now."

August jumps up and adjusts my bed down, hovering over me as he does.

"August."

"Hmmm," he answers.

"Do you think we were broken before we even started?"

My eyes are closing, and I miss his answer as I fall asleep. But I swear I hear him mutter, "We can always be fixed."

"Okay, it's been a week. You're up and moving, and the doctor has cleared you to go home," my nurse says as she comes in, later on that week as I am sitting up on the bed.

"Yeah, about time," Rhianna says, smiling as

she packs up my things.

"What are you doing?" We both turn to August, standing in the doorway. Winter is in his arms.

"She's going home."

He looks to the nurse. "She lives by herself. She will need someone to look after her."

The nurse looks down, red-cheeked, and answers him in a smaller voice than she was just using with us. "The doctor cleared her."

"Then you're staying with me," he states, leaving no room for argument.

"I have a perfectly fine place to stay ... my apartment."

He doesn't listen, just walks over, grabs the bag from Rhianna's arm, and slings it over his shoulder. "Ready?" he asks. My eyes go wide, and I look back to Rhianna for help, but she gives me none.

"August."

He ignores me, looks to Winter, and smiles at her. "Tell Mommy to hurry up. We have to get home and cook dinner." Winter looks me right in the eyes and parrots exactly what August has just said, then leans her head on his shoulder. He smiles in triumph, knowing I won't say no to her.

"Good luck," Rhianna says as she leaves.

"Thanks for nothing," I yell back to her.

"You should use a wheelchair," he says as I make my way to the door.

I scrunch my brows at him. "No, I shouldn't." And with that I ignore him and walk out, August following behind, grumbling under his breath. He directs me to his car and puts Winter in her seat, buckling her in.

As I'm opening the door to get in, he tells me to wait. I stand there, confused, until he shuts the back door and comes to hold my door open and lets me in.

"I could have done that," I whisper as I slide in, but he doesn't reply.

He drives off, and Winter falls asleep in the back seat. We stay silent until we are almost at his place.

"Have you heard anything?" I ask, biting my lip and wondering what's going to happen.

"He tried for bail, but it was denied."

I breathe a sigh of relief.

"I had hardly seen nor spoken to him in five years. For him to come over like that..." I let the thought hang in the air.

"It's over now. I'm sorry I never stopped it."

My eyes flick to him. "This wasn't your fault. You did not put the gun in his hand and squeeze the trigger. That was all on him and his stupid ways."

August grinds his jaw, and I reach over and touch his hand, covering it with mine. He looks down for a quick second, then moves his so our fingers are entwined.

"He's the one who should be dead."

And I know what he's referring to. He means Anderson should be dead instead of Paige. I just nod because no words can express the pain he has from losing her. It killed him so much, he had to leave, and I now understand his reasons.

"You should stay here. Forever," he says as he slows the car and we turn into his driveway. "I have room, and Winter loves it here."

"I have somewhere to live," I tell him. "Plus, you only just separated from Mary. You need time to heal."

"Time is something I don't have. Don't you see that? I've already missed so much. Just move in with me. You don't have to be with me. I'm not asking that of you. I simply want you here, with our daughter."

"That's not something I can do," I tell him honestly.

We can't go from nothing to everything. Things don't work that way. And if they do, they are bound to end up ruined.

And I can't do that.
I don't want us ruined.
I like *us* way too much.

CHAPTER
27

August

Rylee wants to go home, and I want her to stay. But I don't want to force her. I want her to want me as much as I want her. And believe me, I want her. I always have. She is it for me, has been since that day in the bar when I called Rylee by her sister's name, knowing full well what her name was. You see, her eyes, they're different from Rhianna's. Yes, they may look the same in color, but I see something completely different when I look into Rylee's eyes.

Walking around the couch, I see her asleep,

curled up in a ball. A soft snore leaves her mouth as I brush her hair from her face, and her eyes flutter open.

"She's asleep?" she asks.

"She is. Come to bed."

"I'm fine here."

"Don't make me pick you up. I don't want to hurt you." I offer my hand, and she takes it, slowly pulling herself up. When she's standing in front of me, I stay where I am, our bodies so close, not even a matchstick could fit between us right now.

"You can't go from not wanting me, to all of a sudden wanting me, August. You left me. Remember?" Pain is laced in those words.

"I never stopped wanting you. You are the only thing in this world I have ever wanted. Ever."

Rylee's lashes flutter closed, then she looks back up at me. "I had a life planned without you in it."

"You can still plan," I tell her, not moving to give her space. "Just add me to the equation."

"If only life were that simple."

I finally step back, giving her space, and reach for her hand. "Let's go to bed."

She nods, and we walk up the stairs until I get

to my room. She hesitates at the door, and I look back at her. "It's just sleeping. I would never do anything that you didn't want done."

"I'm too sore for anything anyway." Rylee walks past me and goes straight for the bed, still fully dressed. I remove my shirt and put it in the basket, then kick off my jeans. When I turn around, her eyes are glued to my body.

"It's entirely unfair," she murmurs quietly, but I hear her.

I walk over, reach down, and tap the waistband of her shorts. "You want these removed?"

"Yes."

I gently pull and slide them over her ass and down her legs. She lets me, and the only sound is our breathing as I pull them off.

"Do you have a spare shirt?" she asks as she pulls the one she's wearing over her head.

I walk into my closet and come back, handing her one of my shirts. She pulls it on and lies back down.

"Do you think you can cuddle me, August?" She's lying on her side, facing away from me.

"Yes." Without hesitation, I climb into the bed and carefully wrap my arms around her from behind.

"Do you wonder what we could have been?"

she asks.

Her smell envelops me, and all I can do is think of her. She transforms every thought in my head and claims it as hers.

"What we *can* be," I correct her. "Sleep."

Rylee pulls my arm tighter around her waist, and I listen to her breathing even out as she falls asleep.

With her warm and safe in my arms, I'm not far behind her.

"I can feel you staring at me." I open one eye to confirm she is indeed staring at me.

"You look so cute when you're sleeping. Do you know you snore?" The smile that touches her lips makes me open both eyes.

"Do you know you drool?"

Her mouth goes wide, and her eyes enlarge in horror. "I do not."

I look at my arm, and her eyes follow. "I have proof."

"Whatever."

We both go quiet. She smiles shyly at me, and my heart beats hard in my chest.

"Come to Sully and Larry's wedding with me."

"When is it?"

"Next Friday night. Be my date?"

"Date?" she questions.

"Yes, my date."

"Have you ever dated, August Trouble?"

I rub my eyes and flip onto my back, then admit, "No."

"Well, I'm excited." She reaches out and touches my bare chest, and I cover her hand with my own.

"You should probably kiss me now. To seal the deal and all, you know?" I grin and turn to face her to tell her no, that she's sore and the last thing I want to do is hurt her. But she's already there, close enough that when I face her, her lips touch mine ever so softly, tasting me before our mouths open and tongues meet.

I grip her head and hold her in place. One of her hands stays on my stomach while her other one slides down my abs until it arrives at the waistband of my boxers before it slips under to my rock-hard cock.

I break the connection immediately between our lips and shake my head. "Not when you're sore."

She groans but doesn't remove her hand. Instead, she grips me in her fist. My cock twitches, and a seductive smile plays on her lips.

"You should probably kiss me again."

"Woman," I moan and do as she asks, taking her face in my hands and kissing her back. I'm careful that I don't hurt her in any way as I taste something I have missed for a very long time.

Way too long, to be exact.

CHAPTER 28

Rylee

August comes over every day for the next week. I requested to go home after two days of staying at his house. I only get a slight pain when I move wrong or touch the area. Other than that, I'm good.

In two weeks, Jacinta starts work here. Beckham doesn't know who she is, and I don't want to tell him. Beckham doesn't like anyone, and me telling him she is in any way connected to Anderson will only make matters worse. Way worse.

So I plan to leave that well alone.

"Are you really going on a date with him?" Beckham asks as we walk out, and he falls into step next to me. He never leaves work early unless it's for Winter. I have to head home now, feed Winter, bathe her, and make sure she has everything she needs before I take her around to his house.

"Yes, I am."

"I hated him for so long."

We pause when we reach the elevator.

"I know, but you know it was never his fault, right? He loved Paige, and he tried to protect her." We step into the elevator, and Beckham looks directly at me. The caring look in his eyes shows me his feelings. "If something else happened to you..." I lean my head on his shoulder, which is problematic considering how tall he is.

"I'm fine. Really."

"What time?" Beckham asks, shaking me off and assuming his usual stony face.

"I should be there in an hour or two. That work?" He nods and walks to his car, leaving me to fetch Winter.

When I walk into her daycare, I see August sitting down reading a book with her.

"Winter is so cute with him."

Turning to the teacher, I smile. "Yes, they do idolize each other." I walk over and stand next to them. They're so engrossed in the story it takes them both a moment to look up at me.

"Time to go home and get ready for Uncle Beckham's." Winter jumps up straight away and runs to get her bag. When August stands, I see he's dressed in a suit, and my eyes travel the length of him. I smirk when I get to his face and see him already grinning back at me.

"There are children around," he says. "Eyes up here." He taps his face.

"Pish. Please. I'm all better now." I smile and walk out with Winter. August follows us and we head back home. When we arrive, August starts her dinner without me even asking. I take Winter for a shower with me, then dress her so I can start getting ready. August said it's a low-key wedding. Only a few close friends and family will be in attendance. I pull on a black maxi dress covered in pink and purple flowers and pair it with some wedges before I tie my hair up and meet him in the kitchen.

Beckham arrived while I was getting dressed. His hands are in his pockets as he talks to August. I feel August's eyes on me, eating me up as I stand there.

"You sure she is right for the night?" I ask Beckham again.

"Yes, I already told you." Beckham grabs Winter's bag, then turns and walks out, calling Winter as he goes. She gives me a kiss, then August, before she runs off after him.

"I have to get used to their relationship, don't I?" August asks, watching them walk to Beckham's car. It's funny because Beckham has an expensive sports car, but in it right now is a booster seat, which took some convincing for him to put in. I'm sure he hates it, but he does it anyway because of how much he loves Winter and wants her to be safe.

"You do. I love their bond. It's something special." I look back to August. "But *your* bond with her will be different. You are her father, and she knows that." He eyes me. "She asked me, and I couldn't lie. The teacher mentioned you during the week and asked if you were her dad. I replied yes and didn't realize Winter was behind me when I did. I hope that's okay?"

"It's more than okay. I have wanted to tell her, but I wanted to wait until you were ready."

I shrug. "She already asked when she can start calling you Dad. I said she needs to ask you that question." As I turn to walk back into my room, his strong hands grip me on the waist, spinning me around. His lips slam into mine.

I forget to breathe.

I forget to exist outside this moment with him.

Every moment with August is like this.

It's one of the reasons I knew I could never love anyone else the same way I love this man.

He didn't just steal pieces of me. He stole every inch of me and never gave them back when he left. And I never asked for them back either.

August pulls back, his lips a soft pink now from my lip gloss, and I reach up to wipe it away from his lips and smirk. "Maybe I should meet you in the car, so we can get out on time." I laugh.

He nods and walks straight out the door while I reapply my lip gloss.

The wedding was beautiful. Sully and Larry are so in love, and I adore that Larry's family is here to support them. Sully comes over after the ceremony, a wine glass in hand, as we sit at the table next to them, eating a lovely dinner.

"You two are next, right?" he asks with a glint of playful mischief in his eyes. I choke on my food and August taps my back ever so lightly. I manage to wipe my mouth before I look at August.

"The thought of marriage to me makes you choke?" he asks.

Sully smirks but covers his mouth with his

wine glass.

"You've been married," I remind him.

"In a courthouse. We signed papers and walked out."

"Oh." I never asked how or where he was married, figuring it was none of my business. "Noah is handling the papers for the divorce, just so you know. It should be finalized by the end of the month."

"Is Jacinta okay with that?" I ask.

"It's not her I'm worried about. Are *you* okay with that?"

"You two are basically a married couple already. Apart from the sexual tension, which, I might add, is floating around and filling this room to the brim with the way you two keep looking at each other. Have you not had sex yet?" Sully asks, glancing between us.

"The last time we had sex, I fell pregnant," I say to Sully, lifting my own wine glass before taking a sip. I am not even tempted to mention that I was with him not long ago...

"Holy shit." Sully backs away. "You are free to leave. Go fuck. Make more adorable children."

I turn to August. "I don't want any more kids," I tell him, avoiding the talk of sex.

"What if I do?" August asks, amused by my outburst as it plays on his lips.

"It sounds like a *you* problem, not a *me* problem."

"I think we should go. You know, to discuss this in private ... in the bedroom." He stands, pushing his seat back, then calls over to Sully who happily comes back our way.

"We're going. Congrats, man."

Sully nods, the smile never leaving his face, knowing exactly why we're going.

August pulls my chair out and holds my hand as we make our way outside. He opens the car door and lets me slide in before he shuts the door and rounds the hood to jump in on the driver's side. I watch him drive, his concentration entirely on the road until we get back to his house.

"I'm going to kiss you when we get in there, and then I'm going to restrain myself from doing anything else," he tells me. Those forest green eyes, which I have loved for so long, turn on me. His heated gaze roams over me and stops when his eyes lock back to mine. "You're still healing, and I don't want to hurt you. Hurting you hurts me."

"I think I should decide that, right?" I get out of the car and pull my hair out of its bun as he comes up behind me and unlocks the front door, letting me step inside first. As soon as I've crossed the threshold, I spin around and unzip my dress, letting it fall to the floor. Fire burns in his eyes as he shuts the door and locks it behind him.

"Rich girl," he says, shaking his head and biting his bottom lip with a look of lust written in those piercing green eyes.

"I like to be touched. I miss being touched..." I let my hands roam down between my naked breasts and to the top of my panties. "And your touch is what I crave the most. Do you know why that is, August?"

He shakes his head, and I watch as his trousers start to tent where his cock is becoming hard.

"Because only you know how to touch me the way I like." I slip my hand in my panties and begin massaging my clit. "Only you know which spot makes me..." I touch that spot and a moan escapes my mouth. Before I can say anything else, August tears his shirt off and drops to his knees in front of me. He pulls my panties to the side and kisses between my legs, soft then a bite, soft then a bite.

I grip the top of his hair as he gives me the pleasure I so clearly crave.

August knows how to touch me like no other person has ever done before. He is careful where he needs to be, and cruel where I want him to be.

My hands slide down my body to his hair,

gripping hold as he takes me in his mouth and gives me incredible pleasure.

I'm not surprised when it doesn't take long for the pleasure to overtake me. My body starts to shake, but his mouth doesn't stop. His tongue dances on my clit as if he is weaving magic, and believe me, it feels like he is.

Poetic magic perhaps.

My head drops back, and I can't help the thoughts that run through my mind.

He is *it* for me.

August Trouble is literally what makes my world spin. Before everything was in black and white, now it's in real Technicolor. And I could spin forever with him by my side.

"August." His name leaves my lips on a plea, and he pulls away as my knees start to buckle and go weak. The waves of pleasure shoot through me, and I have to remember to breathe. Breathe through everything he's doing to me.

August stands and wipes his mouth before he undoes his trousers and peels them off. Then he's right there before me, in all his naked perfection.

"We have to be gentle..." he says through gritted teeth, "... and that's going to be hard when I want you so fucking bad."

"I'm not breakable," I tell him, smirking. My

hands find his chest and caress his defined muscles. My fingers trail over the body I have missed so much, getting reacquainted with the feel of him.

"No, but you're hurt. And I never want to bring you any more pain than I already have." His words punch me right in the chest, then straight into my heart.

"You did what you thought was right." His rough fingers touch my chin, stroking it before he angles it up and looks me in the eyes. I get lost in his forest green eyes for just a moment, but in reality, it could be an eternity.

"Leaving you never felt right, but my wicked heart told me it was."

"You're back now." I kiss a trail up his chest and throat until my lips meet his and he kisses me back.

August kisses me for all the moments in time he has missed. For the past, that was taken, and for the present, that leads to our future. Then, with greedy hands, I push him back until he drops onto the couch. I straddle his lap, and his hands trail up and down my back, loving me with his touch, claiming me ever so gently.

Those hands could destroy me if they wanted, and I would be helpless to stop them.

"Rich girl," he moans as I slide down on him.

"Mmmm..." It's all I can manage, the ability to

form words temporarily disabled as my brain fills with nothing but August and pleasure.

"I'm afraid I may never let you go again." He bites my neck, and I go slow, wanting to feel him inside me. Wanting to make everything last a few seconds longer than it would normally.

Because all we get are moments.

And I want to steal every one.

From this day forward.

"Fuck," he swears as my hips start grinding faster. I feel him gripping me as he starts to come, and I follow soon after.

My lips find his as my body succumbs to him completely.

CHAPTER
29

August

"Dad." I smile down at Winter, and her nose scrunches up. "Dad," she says again as if testing it on her lips. "I like saying Dad," she says proudly.

And honestly, I fucking like hearing it.

Actually, I love it.

But I keep my lips shut because that word is not about me.

"Winter, hunny, why don't you go pack a bag to spend the night at..." Rylee looks at me, her mouth open, not sure what to say.

"Dad's house," Winter finishes for her.

"Yes, hunny, Dad's house."

Winter runs to her room as Rylee makes a sandwich. She scrapes Vegemite over the bread and then a cheese slice, and I scrunch my nose up at her.

"Please don't pull that face unless you've tried it." Rylee holds it out to me, and I take a step closer because I can't seem to help myself.

"I'm not eating that," I tell her.

"If you want to eat me again, you'll try it."

My lip quirks at her words. "When did you get so feisty?" I lean in and take a bite.

Rylee lets me and smiles when I do. I chew and watch her amused eyes as she stares at me. Waiting. The minute I swallow, I open my mouth slightly and screw up my lips. "That was fucking awful. Absolute shit. But how can I say no when tasting that sweet fucking pussy again was on the line?" Rylee's cheeks flush at my words.

"What's pussy?" We both turn around, and with wide eyes, we stare at Winter. "Maybe I want to taste it too if Dad likes it."

Rylee starts to choke on her sandwich, and I have to remember to stop rapidly blinking from the words that just left her mouth.

"Lassy, love, not the other word," I tell her, trying to cover the mistake with something else, but I fail miserably. Incredibly miserably.

Rylee covers her mouth with her sandwich to hide her grin.

"Mom, can't you come, too? We could watch movies and eat all the popcorn."

"Yeah, rich girl, *eat* all the popcorn." I smirk at Rylee, and her cheeks flush pink.

"How can I say no to you?" Rylee smiles down at our daughter, then pins me with a stare, one that searches my body with those eyes, knowing full well why I want her to come.

What can I say?

I'm a slave to all things her.

Rylee's fingers entwine with mine a week later as we walk through the center of town. We're on the search for ice cream. Tomorrow, Rylee is going back to work, and she is almost completely healed. I study her and can't help but love every inch of her, from the scowl she wears as she stares into the ice cream shop because they don't have the flavor she wants, to the smile that touches her lips when she turns and sees me staring.

"What's going through your head?" she asks

as people walk past and pay us no mind. Winter is with Beckham, as he demanded to have a day with her. And us, well, we are on the hunt for ice cream, and in doing that, we had to head into the city to find the best parlor.

"Just how I missed so much," I tell her honestly. "And how I can't wait to see you naked very soon." My lip twitches and she rolls her eyes with a smile on her face.

"Well, I didn't get married, so you didn't miss much." Rylee turns and looks back to the shop, trying to hide the sadness and disappointment that I know will be emanating from her eyes for me. I step up behind her and wrap my arms around her waist.

Kissing her neck, I murmur, "It wasn't Jacinta I wanted to marry. It was you. It's always been you."

"You can't say things like that," she whispers.

"Why not? It's true."

Rylee shakes her head. "No, because you left me. You. Left. Me. And you married someone else." She turns in my arms, so she's facing me. It's hard not to push her against the glass and have her right here and now, take her, bend her to my will. I have a feeling she would be incapable of stopping me, but I won't. Not in public.

"Do you want to get married? If that's what you want, I will do it. Would that make you happy?"

Rylee pushes at my chest, and I know I've said the wrong thing instantly. "I'm not like *her*. You can't make a deal with me, or just say 'hey, let's get married.' That doesn't appeal to me, and it shouldn't appeal to you either, that is if you love me."

I step back and scrub my hands over my face. When I look back at her, her arms are crossed over her chest.

"Rich girl."

She shakes her head, exasperated. "Do not 'rich girl' me."

Stepping to her, I cage Rylee in with my arms so she can't escape and lean down to whisper in her ear, "When I marry you ... because I will ... you *will* have my last name. I will *not* ask you in any other manner than which you deserve. I was sampling asking now to ease the discomfort you seem to have with the thought that I married someone else." Before she can say another word, my lips cover hers and press hard. She opens her mouth, giving me access, and her hands slide beneath my shirt, her cold fingers splaying on my bare skin.

Someone coughs behind us.

Pulling back, I rest my forehead on hers. "I plan to marry you. I plan to have more babies with you if that's what you want to do, and if not, that's fine as well. I plan to live with you. Fuck, my whole life I have planned around you. And before you, I never had plans. I lived every day as it came. I didn't have a choice. I was destined for one place and one place only. It's because I found you that I never went back. So, rich girl, every other path would have led me back to you. I just happened to get sidetracked along the way."

"August," she says, pulling me in with those wicked, dark eyes.

"Hmmm?"

"I don't want ice cream anymore."

"And what do you want?" I ask.

"You."

"That's something I can easily arrange."

"I hope so," she says, ducking out from under my arm and going back to the car. I follow behind her, and she climbs in the back seat instead of the front. She motions with her finger for me to get in, and I do just that. The minute I close the door behind me, she climbs onto my lap and reaches for my jeans, unbuttons them, and slides her hand in until she has a firm hold on my cock. She slides her hand up and down, all the while staring at me.

"I don't need a ring or marriage," she tells me. "Just you." Rylee pulls up her dress and positions herself over me while she moves her panties to the side. She then slides down on my cock, and when she does, both hands come up and latch on to my shoulders and dig in as she starts to move.

Over the last week, I have let her have control because I've been too afraid of hurting her. And I enjoy it. I appreciate how she demands of me what she wants and isn't scared to take it. But make no mistake, she will be tied to the bed very soon. I will be in total control, and she will bend at my mercy.

She moves, her hips grinding fast, and I halt her, grabbing her hands from my shoulders and putting them behind her back, holding her wrists with one hand. She slows her hips' movement and drops her head back as she takes it all.

No rush, just pleasure.

When she comes, I let go of her wrists, and her head falls to my shoulder while I'm still inside of her.

"I plan to marry you. I plan to keep you forever," I whisper in her ear. I watch as a shiver wracks her body, and a smile touches her lips.

"Forever?" she asks quietly.

"Forever and ever," I promise.

We stay like that for a while, until she crawls off my lap and tells me she wants ice cream. I watch as she gets out of the car, her long dark hair swaying as she does, a smile touching her lips that were made to make my heart rate pick up.

The first time I saw her at that party all those years ago, I knew she was something special, knew she would change me if I let her, but what I didn't expect was that I would let her.

I've fallen hard for the girl whose eyes are as dark as a stormy night sky.

Somewhere along the way, our wicked hearts collided, and the poison remained, coursing just under the surface, waiting to ignite.

We are slaves to each other, and she will always be it for me no matter what.

In this life, and the next.

OTHER BOOKS BY
T. L. SMITH

Kandiland

Pure Punishment (Standalone)

Antagonize Me (Standalone)

Degrade (Flawed #1)

Twisted (Flawed #2)

Black (Black #1)

Red (Black #2)

White (Black #3)

Green (Black #4)

Distrust (Smirnov Bratva #1) FREE

Disbelief (Smirnov Bratva #2)

Defiance (Smirnov Bratva #3)

Dismissed (Smirnov Bratva #4)

Lovesick (Standalone)

Lotus (Standalone)

Savage Collision (A Savage Love Duet book 1)

Savage Reckoning (A Savage Love Duet book 2)

OTHER BOOKS BY
T. L. SMITH

Buried in Lies

Distorted Love (Dark Intentions Duet 1)

Sinister Love (Dark Intentions Duet 2)

Cavalier (Crimson Elite #1)

Anguished (Crimson Elite #2)

Conceited (Crimson Elite #3)

Insolent (Crimson Elite #4)

Playette

Love Drunk

Hate Sober

Heartbreak Me (Duet #1)

Heartbreak You (Duet #2)

My Beautiful Poison (Wicked Poison #1)

My Wicked Heart (Wicked Poison #2)

Find all of her books on
www.tlsmithauthor.com

Made in the USA
Monee, IL
22 August 2022

12152082R00153